D0457800

ALSO BY JEFF VANDERMEER

FICTION

The Strange Bird
Borne
Annihilation
Authority
Acceptance
Area X
The Book of Frog (stories)
Dradin, in Love
The Book of Lost Places (stories)
Veniss Underground
City of Saints and Madmen
Secret Life (stories)
Shriek: An Afterword
The Situation
Finch
The Third Bear (stories)

NONFICTION

Why Should I Cut Your Throat?
Booklife: Strategies and Survival Tips for the 21st-Century Writer
Monstrous Creatures
The Steampunk Bible (with S. J. Chambers)
Wonderbook: The Illustrated Guide to Creating Imaginative Fiction
The Steampunk User's Manual (with Desirina Boskovich)

DEAD ASTRONAUTS

JEFF VANDERMEER

MCD FARRAR, STRAUS AND GIROUX NEW YORK

DEAD ASTRO-NAUTS

FOR ANN, ALWAYS,
ACROSS ALL THE WORLDS

MCD
Farrar, Straus and Giroux
120 Broadway, New York 10271

Printed in the United States of America
First edition, 2019

Library of Congress Cataloging-in-Publication Data
Names: VanderMeer, Jeff, author.
Title: Dead astronauts : a novel / Jeff Vandermeer.
Description: First edition. | New York : MCD/Farrar, Straus and Giroux, 2019. | Series: [Borne series]
Identifiers: LCCN 2019022186 | ISBN 9780374276805 (hardcover)
Subjects: | GSAFD: Science fiction.
Classification: LCC PS3572.A4284 D43 2019 | DDC 813/.54—dc23
LC record available at https://lccn.loc.gov/2019022186

Designed by Abby Kagan

10 9 8 7 6 5 4 3 2 1

Thanks to my first readers, who included, in no particular order, Julia Elliott, Gwynne Lim, Greg Bossert, Ann VanderMeer, Rita Bullwinkel, Amy Brady, Elvia Wilk, Alison Sperling, Timothy Morton, Jonathan Wood, and Jason Sanford. I am indebted to the biology and environmental sciences departments at Hobart and William Smith Colleges for conversations with faculty and students that influenced this novel. I am also indebted to the perspective of the environmentalist Erica Corinne Broderhausen. Thanks to the Bloom Festival 2019 for publishing an excerpt from "Can't Forget" in their program book.

Thanks to the gracious and patient dead astronauts who continue to work on missions for MCD/FSG. May the eel always favor you and no ill eel come to you.

And when I dream
I keep my promises to you
I really do.

—HOT SNAKES

7 *"What version is this?"*

7 *"Zero. It's version zero."*

7 *"Do you trust me?"*

7 *"I do."*

7 *"Do you love me?"*

7 *"I do."*

7 *"Hold on to me, then."*

7 *"I will."*

7 *"Even when I'm not me."*

7 *"I will, Moss."*

0 *"And I will always be there."*
Even before I know you.
Even after I've known you.
Even then.

CONTENTS

DEAD ASTRONAUTS

1. THE DREAM OF THE BLUE FOX

v.1.0

So they ran threaded through the breaches, found the seams. So they ran with a memory of the City without buildings. So they navigated two worlds: the new and the old. When the ancient seabed had been green with reeds and lakes and the low salt-poisoned trees with their thick moss-encrusted limbs upon which they might sleep.

Now they must come to rest on half-collapsed roofs and in the shadows of the great rocks out in the desert. Now they must dream where they could and trust in the lookout who would not sleep. Must trust in how thought danced from mind to mind. How there was nothing but a lightness to that. How they knew each other's will.

They were the color of sand, which might shift and stall, pass between the paws unnoticed, but would never not be

there. Would never become weathered down because it was already what it was meant to become.

One from another in the night they snapped at the winking rescue lights of giant fireflies. Savored the crunch of wing, the collapse of carapace. Let in the coolness of the dark. Played games in the aftermath, searched for hidden water, dug their own shallow wells. Licked at the salt when needed. Mated and had cubs. Sometimes looked up at the stars distant and for a moment contemplated what lay beyond. Even though it meant nothing more to them than the fireflies.

Until Nocturnalia.

Until the blue fox.

For one night there came a flare of blue across the heavens and a nimble quicksilver thought in their heads that was both familiar and strange. They sat at the border between the desert and the City. Hearts pumping fast. Motionless but ready to leap, to run, to bite.

Out across the desert came the Source. At a trot. With a familiar grin of fangs. The blue fox. Larger than them by half. Projecting to them what he wanted to project.

Love. Power. Fate. Destiny. Chance.

Showing them another world. Another way.

But why should they have a leader? Why should they not roam like wild things? For they were wild things. Why should they have a purpose? For they were wild things.

I will tell you why said the blue fox as he approached. *I will tell you why it matters. To you.*

Soon under the glancing moon, the blue fox stood before them. He stood mighty before them. He stood respectful before them. He stood before them.

Came a mighty yipping and barking from the multitudes, the gathered folk that were foxes but not foxes as had been known in the past. For what had a fox been but what a human thought it was?

The blue fox said:

There shall come scavengers to the City from far away. They will call themselves the Company. They shall have no face. They shall have no body at which to strike, but many limbs.

There shall issue forth from the Company beasts and monsters and creatures that shift their form in ways that you cannot imagine. There shall come threats you cannot imagine.

The little foxes seethed, withdrew, seethed around the blue fox, moving like a memory of the sea. Cusp of a new thing, considering what the blue fox showed them.

And by the time the foxes left that place, the blue fox was their leader, and although not one of them could say why this should be, it felt right. It felt true. And in no particulars could it be said that their lives changed in the short-term. In no particulars were they not themselves after. Yet in their hearts they felt the change.

There will be a terrible price to be paid. But I will pay it. If you follow me.

It made them braver. It made them fierce. It focused their thoughts through the prism of the blue fox's mind.

Now their play had purpose.

There shall come three humans across the burning sands . . .

2. THE THREE

v.3.1

i.

came unto the city
under an evil star

A glimmer, a glint, at the City's dusty edge, where the line between sky and land cut the eye. An everlasting gleam that yet evaporated upon the arrival of the three and left behind a smell like chrome and chemicals. Out of a morass and expanse of nothing, for what could live beyond the City? What could thrive there?

Then scuffed the dust, the dirt: A dull boot, a scorpion-creature scuttling for safety much as a human would had a spacecraft crash-landed there. Except the owner of the boot

knew the scorpion was unnatural and thus anticipated the scuttle and crushed the biotech beneath one rough heel.

The boot-scuffer was the one of the three who always went first: a tall black woman of indeterminate age named Grayson. She had no hair on her head because she liked velocity. Her left eye was white and yet still she could see through it; why shouldn't she? The process had been painful and expensive, part of her training a long time ago. Now she glimpsed things no one else could, even when she didn't want to.

Kicked a rock, sent it tumbling toward the thankless dull scrim of the City. Watched with grim satisfaction as the rock, for an instant, occluded the white egg that was the far-distant Company building to the south.

The other two appeared behind Grayson in the grit, framed by that bloodless sky. Chen and Moss, and with them packs full of equipment and supplies.

Chen was a heavyset man, from a country that was just a word now, with as much meaning as a soundless scream or the place Grayson came from, which didn't exist anymore either.

Moss remained stubbornly uncommitted—to origin, to gender, to genes, went by "she" this time but not others. Moss could change like other people breathed: without thought, of necessity or not. Moss could open all kinds of doors. But Grayson and Chen had their powers, too.

"Is this the place?" Chen asked, looking around.

"Such a dump," Grayson said.

"Old haunts never look the same," Moss said.

"Would be a shame not to save it, no matter how shoddy," Grayson said.

“Shall we save it, then?” Chen asked.

“No one else will,” Moss said, completing the ritual.

All the echoes of the other times, what they said when things went well, scrubbing what they'd said when it didn't.

They did not truly speak by now. But thought their speech into one another's minds, so that they might appear to any observer as calm and impassive as the dirt atop an ancient grave.

How could they dream of home? They saw it continually. They saw it when they closed their eyes to sleep. It was always in front of them, what lay behind, overwriting the places that came next.

Chen said they had arrived at the City under an evil star, and already they were dying again and knew they had no sanctuary here—only accelerant. But the three had been dying for a long time, and had vowed to make their passage as rough, ugly, and prolonged as possible. They would claw and thrash to their end. Stretched halfway to the infinite.

None of it as beautiful or glorious as an equation, though. All of it pushed toward their purpose, for they meant, one of these days or months or years, to destroy the Company and save the future. Some future. Nothing else meant very much anymore, except the love between them. For glory was wasteful, Grayson believed, and Chen cared nothing for beauty that declared itself, for beauty had no morality, and Moss had already given herself over to a cause beyond or above the human.

“While we're only human,” Grayson might joke, but it was because only Grayson, of the three, could make that claim.

This was their best chance, the closest to the zero version, the original, that they might ever get, this echo of the City. Or so Moss had told them.

Grayson, the restless one, the leader, if leader they had, took point, and her blank eye was her gun, her hand her gun, and no aim ever truer. But all three had restless, dangerous thoughts. All three had minds that reeled from the imprint of strange constellations and distant coordinates. Hell lay behind them on that map—blood and murder and betrayal.

And because the three were home, and because they strode toward the City, which was everywhere the property of the Company, the enemy came for them. Tripped an invisible wire.

Apparitions sprang from the sand, dust devils formed like sand but not sand that took the shape of vast monsters with glittering eyes: Bio-matter with nanites instead of intent, to bring down upon them punishment for their rebellion. A digging gap-jawed leviathan that ate the soil and vomited it back out, transformed. A flying creature with many wings that blotted out the sun. Claws and fangs were to be expected and a lust to kill, grown more corporeal with each staggering step the creatures took, so that what might seem ghost matter or star matter gathered with a great soughing sigh and low guttural groan as it became strong where once it had been weak.

Only Moss ever found them sympathetic, and that was because she was closer to them in her flesh than to Grayson or Chen. Phosphorescent, dripping a mist of near-weightless

biomass in emerald and turquoise torrents, as if they had emerged not from desert but from some vast and ancient sea. The brine of them hit the three in a wave, and the taste of them registered Paleo-Mesozoic, worthy of the respect one gave to old bones in a museum.

But these monsters had been made to combat some other enemy than the three, and not a one of the three hesitated in their step or paid these apparitions any heed—ignored the terrifying sounds, the slavering jaws, the shadow rippling across the heated sand—and when the molecules of the three met those of the defenders, the defenses fell away and again became like sand.

Sometimes this was not the case.

Sometimes, when they were not the three but just the one or the two or in some other guise and thus weakened, the sentinels devoured them, ripped their flesh and cracked their bones. Rendered their corpses down into dust, and then quarantined the dust and salted it, as if knowing how dangerous even the DNA of ghosts could be. They had taken readings, logged the evidence of this, knew it to be true.

Here, in this City, there came a second wave in the form of a giant lizard and Grayson dealt with the surprise with a leap and a swipe of her arm, for there appeared a blade at the end of her hand and then a red line across a scaly throat. This lizard erupting from the sand was not biotech but natural bred and thus natural dead in disposition.

Yet it hid the preternatural, for one limb of the lizard made as if to flee into the sky and became a wing that might flap and soar. A wing turning into a full-fledged bird that might report back to the Company.

But for Chen, who whipped his left arm up toward the heavens and allowed that part of him that identified as "hand" to leave him, to spin up to the wing as a sharp spinning star and to intercept the flying thing—and to shatter it to pieces, which fell like shards of green glass or some brittle candy.

While the star of his hovering hand shone golden there in the great empty sky, like a beacon.

The monsters were gone; they had passed the first trial. Yet it was different than before. More difficult. Each of them felt that, in some hard-to-define way.

"They will track us."

"They always track us."

"The duck with the broken wing?"

"Already here."

Sometimes it took longer, but true: The duck with a broken wing watched their approach from a dusty pool in which a dark smudge was all that remained of water. More reptilian than duck. Saurian. Teeth. Semblance of a duck. But only from afar. Up close, all that registered was *monster.* Sometimes they called it "the dark bird."

The duck always waited for them in the City. The one constant, like a fixed compass, one that was broken or made to be false. The duck waited for them through all the versions, all the years.

The mantra went: "First the duck, then the fox," and, lately, "then the fish." (Or, sometimes, "the manta," which soared off above the dry seabed like a memory of plenty.)

The first question, when they arrived: "Is the duck on our side or against us?"

For if the duck was against them, disaster became more

likely. Perhaps the duck had seeded the earth with the monsters just defeated, but worse were the times when it stood before them upon first approach, analyzed their nature, and disgorged more specific weapons, and then they knew the duck truly opposed their purpose.

A presence existed in the ground below the duck, shadowed the duck from below and gave it power. They had never glimpsed this something, only felt it, like a curse.

"The duck is on our side here," Moss said.

"You sound uncertain," Chen said, other arm extended like the weapon it was, ready to inflict his mark upon the duck.

"It is at least neutral," Moss conceded, but she still did not sound sure.

Which concerned Chen, concerned Grayson.

In the past, Moss had always known and was always right, they had discovered. When the duck appeared smooth in Moss's mind, the duck would not hurt them. When the duck appeared rough there, the duck would hurt them. That was the only way she could explain it.

To Grayson the duck before them manifested as a tiny sun aswarm with rippling maggots of cascading light. Her special eye could not analyze it or penetrate that blinding aura, could not thus break down the elements of the duck. Could not say whether it was a pillar of salt or a cauldron of flesh. No percentages scrolled across her vision.

This was itself relief from the sight she could not now turn off, something gone faulty, the world so much incoming data that it was no data at all, and she must always recuse herself, tamp and withdraw when she could, for her sanity.

But Grayson welcomed the duck with the broken wing because it reminded her that even something broken could have a use. That nothing should be wasted. And that what might appear broken might in fact be whole.

"Then the foxes first," Grayson said. "We parlay with the foxes."

The ritual. If ever broken, what else might break?

The three picked up their equipment and as one they advanced across the sands into the City. While they felt as one the weight of the duck's skeptical eye, recording all.

Their shadows were long and dangerous, flickered and seemed to catch fire as the light faded, and still they trudged forward, inexorable as any three people who had loved one another fiercely and seen nothing but the best in one another. Across so many years, and now with nothing left to lose.

They had failed in the last City, and the one before that, and the one before that. Sometimes that failure pushed the needle farther. Sometimes that failure changed not a thing.

But perhaps one day a certain kind of failure might be enough.

ii.

they needed no fire
for the fire burned
within all of them

Chen could see bits and pieces of the future, "but only in equations." A frequent lament. Numbers could attack the flesh, the will, but rarely built it up. Morale for them never lay in the numbers. He made poetry out of his premonitions, his equations, because they'd proven useless to him as fact, because he was never sure whether he was actually seeing the past. A past.

Chen liked to play the piano and to down a hearty meal with a beer. Meals because he spent prodigious energy keeping his form. The piano because it made him remember to be careful—how watchful he must be of his own thick

fingers. Or this is what he said, "It makes me limber-er," when mostly it was a link to his history. Or what had been implanted in him as history.

There had been little enough of either lately. Pianos and hearty meals. He must take his sustenance from the molecules of the air with which he often felt interchangeable, and he compared notes with Moss, because their moves through fluid states were similar, even if his was a kind of fight against evaporation or ejection and hers an overabundance of accretion, a building up.

Flesh was quantum. Flesh was contaminated, body and mind.

Chen dealt in probabilities on one side of his brain and impossibilities on the other. Because the probability was always that he would disintegrate into his constituent parts sooner rather than later. He had come to think of himself as a complex equation and a symphony both, and, really, what was the difference?

The equation of the Company eluded Chen, perhaps because he had been lost within it once upon a time. Or as he said sometimes, the system abhors *source*, makes its mapping into a maze, a mockery, and the more you think you understand it, the more you are colonized by it. And lost.

As they walked, suspicious of the shadows within every husked building:

"It was never real."

"It was real." Chen or Moss, it didn't matter.

"Not real in the sense of lasting."

"Nothing is real, then."

"Real enough."

Real enough was the anchor that kept them from falling apart. Through all the versions.

The glowing star of Chen's hand had begun to burn before the drift, so that it did not plummet but, light, hollowed out, it caressed the air as ash in hand-form, disintegrated before it could reach the ground. Almost as if the hand could not believe in its own engineering. He would grow another by morning.

Yet still he felt the hand as it floated, as it drifted, as it became nothing. Loved the weight and certainty of that dissolution.

The hand laid bare the one who had created it, along with Moss: Charlie X, whom Chen thought of as the missing fourth member of their party. Vain hope. Nothing across the versions to support it. Nothing that could have registered on Grayson's radar, just in the form of a bullet she would like delivered to Charlie X's brain. Even though it was too late.

Charlie X was on some part of the blackboard that had been smudged and no one could solve the equation now. Just knew the original answer had been incorrect.

"What's my point?"

"Are you losing your point?"

"Your point is your defense."

"I still have three points to use."

Were they all losing the point along the way?

If so, Moss least of all because she didn't have the luxury. She was the map, the way in and the way out, the leader of the heist and its blueprint.

Chen's equation was a wall of circles with plus signs between them, and then some basic geometry that proved he was more than the sum of his parts. Held together by math.

But Moss? Messier. Moss liked, well, moss—and lichen and limpets and sea salt and the beach and guessing the geological scale of things. And strawberries—she loved strawberries now that there were none anywhere they went. Also, Moss liked to rescue whatever animal or plant needed it. She believed they had earned it.

Moss lived based on a kind of crime that Chen had witnessed part of but neither had shared with Grayson, as if it were a wound that would bleed out if offered up. Moss kept that wall high and inviolate; for someone who shared herself so utterly, how could Grayson begrudge this one withhold?

Yet sometimes, Grayson's bad/good eye gleaned hints, the eye so exposed to the alien that it had shut down and opened up, both. Grayson's eye saw: Moss through a swirl of snowflakes, emerging from a tunnel, emerging from a burning shed, as if she leaked memories without her knowledge. Or was this something she projected onto her? How to make sense of that?

For Chen, Moss was a wall of circles or zeros tumbling over one another, and from each a different Moss peered out. That kept being divided by themselves until there was no room for the rest of the equation and the parentheses grew into vines and cracked the blackboard and made math into something that could never be solved. While Moss escaped through one of the circles. For Moss could bud another Moss off her big toe if she liked—as she was fond of saying.

Chen had been beholden to Moss's kindness, in ways Grayson would never understand. You had to be there. You couldn't conceive. Empathy wasn't enough. Imagination wasn't enough.

By contrast, Grayson was a single circle from which radiated calculations like the sun's rays and a latticework of numbers between each ray. She liked to be as direct as a fist to the face. She had survived that way out in space for so many years that there was no other solution for her. She knew the stakes of their mission because she'd had so few choices before Chen, before Moss. Chen tried not to diagram her or turn her into poetry, even though it was in his nature. Did not want to solve her, for fear she'd tumble like Moss's zeros, but, not used to it, shudder apart, disintegrate. No matter the grim set of her jaw.

Chen, Moss, Grayson. They each only used one name now. Had been winnowed down, become too familiar, had not the need nor the want for the territory of two names. When encamped, they lay heedless and seamless huddled all three together. Hard to pry apart for the comfort of it, the touch of another. They needed no fire, for the fire burned within, warmed them even in the deepest cold. And the source was Moss.

"Good night, Moss."

"Good night, Chen, Grayson."

Just a mutter from Grayson, but they knew she loved them.

Each had had the experience of self-annihilation. Chen had killed Chen. Moss had absorbed Moss. Grayson had killed them both. Moss had killed Chen, Chen Moss. Thus

their intimacy had become exponential, along with their sadness and their regret. And it was cocooned within that, that they lay together, so close, to treasure the Chen, the Moss, the Grayson, that still lived.

While all three could feel the duck with the broken wing watching over them from afar. For better or worse.

The dark bird.

iii.

the way his face yet reflected nothing of terrible experience

The City and the Company went by many different names in the Splinters, as Chen put it. In the Mains, it was just City and Company, as the Company preferred, the edges rounded off; no purchase. In the Mains, the risks were greater, but so were the rewards. Splinters could sting, distract, and that was all.

But versions of the City weren't the only variable that Chen calculated, that Moss embodied. Time was a second variable, and time was not inexorable. Some Times it seemed as if they sped forward into their own future, and those were the worst moments.

The City glittering upon the plain inviolate—and terrible

for it, the Company building grown so fat and thick and all tributaries leading into it, with no wastelands or outliers. Smell of blood. Just the Company and no City at all. These maze-versions they turned their backs on in haste, turned their backs on their own mortality and uselessness. For nothing could be gained, only lost.

The City, smoldering upon the plain violate—and terrible for it, the Company building dead husk and the tributaries dried up, all wasteland and outliers. Just the City and no Company at all. While shape-shifting creatures with camouflage like cuttlefish and chameleons expressed as enormous wildflowers transformed whatever raised its head from refuge. The smell of death as a rich, velvety sigh.

These versions they turned their backs on slowly, after days in their contamination suits, careful not to breathe the air. You could regroup in such a place, but you would find no sanctuary, nor an adversary. You could be lulled, or culled, and a lull was like death in the end. Woken from a dream of blossoms into a swaying disintegration.

For that was what bodies wanted: To come to rest. To know no more.

This City was like all the Cities: the observatory to the northwest, the factories to the northeast, against the polluted sludge path that was the river; the vast complex of pockmarked half-derelict apartments to the south of the factories, where the Company housed the workers; and to the southwest the white smudge of the Company building.

What varied most was the expanse between factories and Company, across the diagonal, the ancient seabed. Sometimes this was an utter ruin. Sometimes an estuary rich with holding ponds that led to the encircling river. Sometimes it served as satellite to the Company and, at least at first, industrious if not prosperous. People in numbers, making a sort of living, perhaps even selling food they'd grown to those who came out from the Company.

Grayson in particular distrusted those visions. Everything the Company did destroyed someone, killed someone, even if it helped someone else. All the rest was subterfuge, and no suit to protect against it.

"That wasn't there in mine."

"Was in mine."

"In mine there were only mines. There."

And there and there and there.

Not mines that could blow you up. Mines that could destroy your mind, change your body. Make even the thought of you never exist.

A dark joke. An old joke. Useful to remember, until you could no longer remember . . . anything.

Other times, they moved backward and the Company appeared in stages of construction, with such activity and so many guards that they could not even comprehend the depth of the danger and challenge before them. In that false promise you could lose your self, could be convinced the futures were glorious . . . if you hadn't already seen the futures.

Everything that promised glory become gory, spreading death underneath, death preferring to dive before erupting back up at the end of days.

Thus Moss, who used Chen's equations to hone her internal compass, so that her foldings in on herself spared the three the impossible ones and chose only those Cities where the bitter possibility of collapse, the cusp of the possible, provided them with a corridor, a moment.

While Chen, bound by Moss, would calculate rates of decay and acceler-deceleration. Would add in relative unknowns like the cataclysm/catechism of the duck, other Chens, the likelihood of one day meeting a hostile Moss, or meeting another Grayson at all.

What it would mean to meet up with a Charlie X who had not become deranged, expunged his memory. What it would mean for Chen not to hate Charlie X or to remember the feeling of Charlie X's gaze upon him. Moving backward to a point where Charlie X would be young and almost featureless in his innocence, the way his face reflected nothing yet of terrible experience.

What Chen never added to the equation.

What Charlie X, in rags, had told him, as something clicked into place behind his eyes. Would click off again, for in those days and those versions Charlie X could never hold on to his self for long.

That one time. In that one place. With Moss and Grayson preoccupied and Chen a fortress-sentinel.

"I remember you. I remember you. I remember you. You were just a dream I had. A dream I made. That's all you are."

Chen had trembled, tamped down the urge to dissolve

and in that dissolution take Charlie X into the dark with him.

For that would be surrender.

Moss had put forth the rules to govern Chen's more useful equations. Moss's "tidal pool rules," which included: Stay still, be small, bring the right camouflage, know good hiding places, become a symbiote or parasite, be poisonous or venomous, be able to regenerate body parts.

If you wanted to survive, reduce all motion to zero over long stretches of time. Trust the current. The current. The current. The species already there. How at high tide the water rippled across all of the tidal pools, even those that had been inviolate, their own tiny kingdoms, before.

If this were the purest City. The one that most rippled through all the others and the Source. If this was the one, then the effect would be greatest here.

But: Be tiny, be motionless. Take your time. Perhaps it would not be the first wave or even the thousandth. Because direct was defended. You contaminated the wall of globes inside the Company, then went to the Source. The portal wall, the magic mirror that led back to where the Company came from. You let it trickle in, like a slow-acting poison that was actually:

Life, again.

She could feel herself, sometimes, using the tidal pool rules to do the things she wasn't doing *here*. Phantom sensations. Of standing in the ravine. Of watching her doppelgänger set off, with Chen by her side.

Memory of Grayson turning to her and saying one of these three things:

"This time. This time. I feel it."

"Someday. We'll go back to your tidal pools."

"How many times has it been now?"

Say a number that felt low. That felt hollow.

Like one of Chen's equations was screaming to get out. Like one of Chen's creatures, trapped in the wall of globes.

iv.

for you cannot give us
what we already have

In this City, as in all Cities, the three knew they would find the foxes. Moss loved the foxes, while Grayson suspected them—thought them already too clever, believed, perhaps, the foxes had led to their failures, as much as the insidious nature of the Company had.

Chen had no opinion, for in his calculation the foxes must always be part of the plan. So he wasted no emotion on them one way or the other.

On a cracked dead bridge splayed in segments across a riverbed of rocks and weeds, the fox met them. They had been clambering across the gully, headed southeast, toward the Balcony Cliffs apartment complex. They wore now their

camouflage, so that they appeared only as a glimmer against whatever backdrop they moved across. *Faery mode,* Moss liked to call it.

In a sense, the fox had ambushed them by taking the high ground of the bridge. This startled them. It had never happened so soon, or in this place.

The blue fox stood perfect-still, regarding them. It was as large as a wolf and Grayson felt the threat of its regard. Could see with her eye the peculiarities of its brain. Just could not tell if the fox had been born that way or tinkered with.

"You are a long way from home," the blue fox said.

"This is our home," Moss replied.

"Not all of you. Not this City. Our City."

"The Company's City."

"Not forever."

Moss was their receiver, and it was through Moss that Chen and Grayson heard her parlay with the blue fox.

"Will you accept a gift from us?" Moss asked.

"I accept no gifts from strangers."

"But we aren't strangers. You know us."

Moss was letting the blue fox into her mind. The farther into that labyrinth the fox explored, the more of the gift the fox would receive. For it would understand their mission, gain more understanding of the Company, and also see how the foxes had helped them across so many Cities. That was the hope.

(What bled through, into the head? Where did they travel all unknowing? This in Moss's mind as disturbance, regis-

tering in Chen as a possibility: v.2.1 = 2.2 + 2.3 + 3.0 + the things that could pull a mind apart if examined close up.)

"Neither shall I set foot on strange paths without a map," the fox said or thought, and in real time it was neither but an image the fox showed Moss—of the fox come to a halt at the entrance to a dark green maze of vines, and the maze was Moss and the fox would not enter the maze. And Moss put this image into words for Grayson, for Chen.

Words ripped smooth by repetition. What Moss had said many times before: "The Company will kill you without our help."

"The Company already kills us, and yet we are here."

All around, from every hiding place, peered the sandy-colored small foxes that were the blue fox's comrades.

"We can make it easier, faster, for you."

The fox considered that, looking out over the City as if the fox would rule the City one day.

"I will give you this much: There is no Moss in this City. No Moss at all. You should consider that before all else." Moss by then was a conduit as well as a person, and even as a person she was an accumulation of Mosses, all of whom lived inside her. Every time Moss encountered another Moss, across timelines, they merged, and she had become more powerful because of it.

Then the fox trotted off the bridge, out of sight, and his followers melted away as if they had never been there.

"That has never happened before," Chen said. He had noticed how the fox looked covetous at Moss, as if she were a tasty morsel. That had not happened before, either.

"Give it time," Moss said, even though Time was a joke. Even though they had less of it with no Moss in the City. No new partner, no new joining.

"How much time do we have?" Grayson asked.

(What came back to Chen was how 7 became both lucky and finite, not a door but a wall. Without an anchor at 6.999999999999. But the fox was the master of it and thus in a way Chen could not see in the numbers . . . their master, too.)

As they met the fox ever earlier, so too would the Company be drawn to them that much faster. This they knew. And Moss knew one thing more the other two did not: that she would see the fox again, soon.

I think you are beautiful, Moss thought hard, at the space the fox had disappeared into. *I think you have always known the future. I think this time I might trust you.*

But she always had done that in the past, too. Because she meant it.

Where had the blue fox come from? The vexing question, the one they had stopped trying to answer. Moss said that the blue fox had not been born in the Company or borne by the Company, or they had so forgotten it that there was no residue. A rogue lab, Chen guessed. Or some spontaneous mutation. Neither probable.

Moss believed: The blue fox was aware of its brethren across all the paths. Moss believed: The blue fox often knew them before first encounter.

Once, Grayson, after analyzing the blue fox and finding only . . . fox . . . pressed the creature.

The fox replied, "I came from where you come from, Grayson. I come from *up there*."

The sky. The stars. The leap of startled recognition in Grayson before she realized the fox was joking. That the fox was telling her she had been *read*, down to her core.

"How do you know?" Grayson had asked. Could not help that reveal.

"You stink of space," the fox said. "You stink of stale air and the burn and countdowns to false zeros, and places not of Earth."

But Grayson thought the fox lied and there was some other reason.

Chen said: Any theory at this point made as much sense, since no theory made sense. That the fox could be inhabited by an alien intelligence. Or it could be a particularly devious AI wormholing back under the power of a self-made destiny. If the paths were open, porous, then other sorts of doors could open as well. Even though Grayson, the only astronaut among them, said aliens had never been encountered by humankind out in the universe. That human beings never mastered AI.

Grayson, uneasy every time, instinct telling her she knew the blue fox from somewhere. Always on the cusp, never able to recall. Distrusting the emotion behind it, careful to keep the fox at arm's length.

The probability was that they would never know. The way most never knew half of anything and had to be content.

"Catch me if you can," the blue fox sometimes said to Moss in joyous reverie. "Catch me if you can."

But they never could.

V.

the first glimpse
was always the most fatal

Only Chen had ever worked for the Company. Some version of it he had left far behind on the map. And so, the first glimpse of the Company building each time was always the most fatal for him. The trauma of it had been known to pull him apart at the seams, it left to Moss to hold him together, for he had the power to dissolve into the sky almost against his will, leave Grayson and Moss on their own, nothing ever his problem again.

Before the tidal pool rules, the three had smashed in the front door of the Company. They had laid siege. They had attacked from afar, through proxies. They had lured Company lackeys into sabotage. They had led uprisings of bio-

tech. They had done this and they had done that. They had been wounded and changed and poisoned and defeated too many times, only got out because of Moss. All the Mosses. Could only regroup because of her.

Had to wait. Try more circuitous ways. Come back much later. After the damage had mostly been done. Irredeemable. Irreparable. Yet they still meant to repair it.

Each time: What next? What now?

Each time, the obstacle seemed more insurmountable.

Chen: "Couldn't you find a future that's a paradise, where we could live out our days together?"

But that was a joke. Because Chen knew none of those timelines contained a Moss, a Chen, a Grayson. Because those timelines did not exist. The Company had tick-engorged itself across all timelines.

This was the problem. You could try to live out your days and years in some remote corner, but even that place would be blighted by the Company, by what happened in the City. They would find you, in time. You would be reminded of your own unwillingness to fight against your fate. The three would become one and one and one, and then none.

Grayson: "There will be a next time."

Moss never replied. She would be thinking of what she had received from Grayson because she loved her, too much. How without Grayson she would not have known to resist. Because Moss had been too close in, too close to Charlie X and, by extension, the dark bird. How Grayson had been like original sin, how Moss was now more fully herself than before.

That they might next succeed. That failure might no

longer be about a semblance of the future. That, in the end, they were three, not an army.

The Company always looked basically the same: whether an enormous white egg or a vast gray triangle or a ziggurat or a series of spires, like a fractured cathedral. Holding ponds for biotech rejects always hunched up against the side, a convenient hell or purgatory, full of dying life, and then lines of invisible defenses across the wasteland beyond. Sometimes things flew through the air that should not have been able to fly, molecules of iridescent blue and green that scintillated and changed shape, ever vigilant.

This version retained the white-egg structure but had curved lines running through the architecture so that it resembled a giant egg slicer with a metal egg sliced within it. A lazy riddle interrogating itself about some other, unrelated question.

This version had propagated the holding ponds across the entire expanse of what was normally desert, and still was, in a sense.

"How did It escape?" Grayson would ask as they stared at the Company.

"We never escaped; It was always there."

"Can It be put to the good?" Grayson would ask.

"No, It cannot. It must be burned to the ground."

"But could we persuade It?"

"Only if you could find a human heart to persuade."

"Only if you could find something *other* than a human heart."

“What will replace It if we succeed?”

“Anything is better.”

But without the Company, they could not have fought the Company.

But this made them at times suspicious of their own three selves.

But they had no choice now but to go on.

In this version, birdsong filled the City, but it was just an echo of nanites created to give the illusion of bird life through ghost calls.

“What will you miss?” Grayson would ask, already knew the answer.

I’ll miss you.

vi.

no one should feel responsible for the whole world

Grayson's past lay very far from home, always sending data and signals without knowing if they made it back. Just one of three vessels forging ahead. Two destroyed by asteroid strike. Her crew dead from all the ways space could murder you: lack of resources, bad decisions, disease, freak injury, the cosmic scale, sun flares, infighting.

Reaching the outermost point, or at least the farthest Grayson could bear. In a suit, looking at rock, rock underfoot. Caressed the outline with one thick glove. Unsure if the formation was the fossil of some alien intelligence, the suggestion of a helmet, of a face. Or just a coincidence, an outline she wanted to see. Would never know.

Feeling in an irrational way that she was looking at her fate if she continued outward bound. Weary. Sick of no grass, no trees. No horizon other than the dark or artificial light. Paltry samples. Paltry evidence.

Knowing that humanity was alone. That even a sea of water could not produce advanced life-forms unless the exact conditions were right. That she didn't in the end care for the microscopic depiction of life. That bacteria warring with bacteria could not evoke in her any kind of awe, that she should stop taking samples of water traces.

She tried to feel for a tremor or warmth in the stone beneath her glove, but the fabric was too thick for anything but the pulse of her own breathing.

Time to return.

Only to then spend a century finding her way home, through all the strange wormholes in the universe. Come to think of it as a useless mission. Come to think of herself as a ghost during that time, lost among the stars and star matter, haunting herself, haunting dead space, haunted by her many selves. Left behind: the dead crew, buried beside the fossil that might be in her head.

Did she deserve to live after the death of her crew? She had no answer, had decided for no good reason that the atoms of which she was made were not yet ready to disperse to form someone or something else.

Thus, Grayson wandered alone and in her own thoughts, at times in danger and at times held in thrall to such cosmic places full of wary (cold) wonder that she could not find the words, and so words fell away from her for a time . . . because they were useless.

Fell away along with so much else that by the time she found the moon base, she would not have recognized rescuers as fellow human beings.

If there had been anyone living on the moon base.

If it wasn't clear all the astronauts were dead.

If she hadn't known home still lay below her.

Grayson returned to a version of the City that held no life. The blackened, flame-eaten forms of people and animals were strewn everywhere. Caught in mid-flight or huddled in corners. The runneling of flesh that forced some flush against the ground, as if returning to the earth might save them.

Fire and chemicals formed a kind of haze over the bodies, an unholy mist. Hiding and revealing and hiding again as it lingered over the dead. As if the Company had sent the mist to hide its crimes.

Roamed that landscape in shock, unaware of just how much time had passed since she had gone into space. Roamed the City as an astronaut might, still in her suit, in constant contact with the life pod.

Grayson had had perhaps a decade of solitude and air left at the base to look down on Earth's ravaged face and try to convince herself that all would one day be better. But instead she'd returned to Earth, burning enough of the pod's remaining fuel on reentry that she could never go back. Her reasons were sound enough: She felt too alone, more alone than just being one person. Too much carnage in memoriam there.

Eye reporting data dispassionate, she had sorted through

the City's wreckage much as a parent might go through a child's messy room. A child missing or passed away. What was valuable. What had been cast aside. What overused. But unable to put it back in order.

In space, discipline meant life or death. Here, there had been no penalty for freedom until the end.

In the twisted remains of the Company building, Grayson found evidence that some had survived and fled west. So she had taken her life pod west, headed for the coast, adrift and aimless. Or maybe not so aimless. What Grayson had planned to do there, she did not know. Perhaps she would have explored until the pod's fuel ran out. Perhaps she planned to die. Perhaps she had some better idea that never came to pass.

But it was there she found a treasure, beneath the broken pink stucco archway that once greeted tourists to a marine amusement park. In its crumbling state, the broken-down cement walls and rising seas had conspired to create artificial tidal pools full of strange life.

Tending to them was Moss.

Grayson found Moss early in the morning, the air fresh enough that she had taken off her helmet. Moss crouched by a tidal pool, cataloging its contents, regulating temperature, encouraging some organisms, discouraging others.

Moss presented ethereal. She presented as naïve, with green eyes that blazed at Grayson as she turned from her crouch, startled at the appearance of this sudden visitor.

Moss had not spoken to another person for months.

Grayson recognized a fellow explorer; she saw in those tidal pools an infinity. Stars reflected there.

"You don't come back often," Moss said. "Sometimes I search for you. But most times you die up there."

"I don't know what that means." Soon enough, she would.

"And I'm sorry," Moss said. Staring so nakedly at Grayson that she looked away.

"For what?"

"That you've seen so much you loved destroyed."

"Hasn't everyone."

"You're an astronaut," Moss said, turning back to her work. "The scale is different."

"We each handle what we can."

"No one should have to feel responsible for the entire world."

Grayson had no answer to that. She considered Moss again. There was a hard edge to Moss, she decided, despite her empathy. What some might call hidden depths. Nothing simple about a person who loved the sea so much she couldn't live without it. Nothing simple about Moss, as Grayson discovered over the next few weeks: cheerful, bright-eyed, optimistic. All of that was difficult; pessimism was easy.

But Moss was purely tactical, tending to her tidal pools. Perhaps Grayson could convince her to be strategic. Once she understood the woman. Although, for a time, it was Moss who convinced Grayson. For a time, Grayson was content living by the sea.

That first day, when Grayson couldn't meet Moss's gaze,

she already knew she had fallen in love. Didn't know Moss had taken human form that first day just for her.

And, in the end, it was Moss who found the way, who had always known the way.

Who was the way.

vii.
by these signs
they knew they were home

The Balcony Cliffs building was much as Chen remembered it—so much so that Moss and Grayson went on ahead to ensure that Chen did not already live there. But Chen's old apartment was empty, rich with trash and giant silverfish. The silverfish danced and paraded and showed no fear, as if the three truly were ghosts.

Moss didn't consider the apartment abandoned. She had always loved seeing silverfish. While they offended Grayson's sense of a recoverable future. It was a visceral reaction—her brain always reminded her that every living thing was sacred now. That any life was a good sign.

"In the end, the silverfish shall inherit the Earth," Moss

said, content. "And they shall build towers in the desert and create a great civilization." For that was one of the myths told in the City.

But the point was: No Chen that they could find, and the fox had told Moss that no Moss grew here, in the City. Perhaps Moss grew farther afield, but this was no help to them.

Grayson had yet to encounter another Grayson in their travels, felt an irrational sense of loneliness when the other two told tales of their doubles. Because what no Grayson meant was that she had perished across most timelines before she made it back to Earth. Because no Grayson could flourish out there for long. A *gloved hand across unforgiving stone.*

Chen and Moss both welcomed finding the Balcony Cliffs' swimming pool again, deserted and full of brackish water without much alive in it. Moss would fix that, not because it affected the mission but because it was in her nature. Because she always hoped to leave things behind that were better than she had found them.

They would claim an empty apartment near the southern edge of the Balcony Cliffs, with an ease of exit toward the ravine that served as preamble to the Company lands. They would be silent and incognito and try to blend in with the others who lived in that space.

"I lived here in mine."

"In mine, I never knew about this place. I lived in the ruined observatory. In the basement. Before I met Moss."

"I visited a friend here, once."

"You had a friend? Doubtful."

A sculpture of a giant bird. The corpse of a dog. A ruined dollhouse.

By these signs they knew they were home.

Their tenth City.

After the Balcony Cliffs' attack beetles had been repulsed, after the scavengers received the message, the three regrouped behind a door blocking off a corridor near the southern entrance. Easily defendable. The door's graffiti featured laughing foxes playing in the desert, each with but a single eye. Chen drew in the second eye on each to balance the equation. Moss reinforced the microbial sensors. There should be no tickle, no trace so light that Moss should not know it in time.

Grayson distrusted the lack of resistance; they had repulsed multitudes in past versions. But though she trained her eye across beams, blueprints and ghost layers bursting across her line of sight . . . she could parse no threat beyond the usual.

Still . . .

"We should move up our timeline," Grayson said.

"But not blind. Not from panic."

"It's not panic. It's common sense."

"What if the fish is stubborn? What if the fish resists?"

"I'll go," Chen said. "I will convince the fish."

"No," Moss said. "It must be me or some part of me."

"Then I will stand watch."

"We must just go in and do what we came here to do."

"I'll go," Chen repeated, with the force of a slammed door.

But the door had already been shut. Grayson and Moss ignored him.

Soon they would need the blue fox to say yes to them. They would need to be sure the duck with the broken wing didn't interfere.

Soon, too, their faery mode might not be enough. Sometimes they had to wear their contamination suits. Depending on Moss's senses, Grayson's eye, Chen's prophecies. What did contamination mean in this City, and which way did it flow?

Each Company building was different. But recon had diminishing returns and too many risks. So they rehearsed their plan, with the aid of the old dollhouse found by Grayson (once again). The Company had seven floors, but it was still easier to visualize using dolls and furniture and rooms than diagrams scratched in the dirt. Some things never changed.

They must get some version of Moss inside the Company building, to compromise the portal wall, to infiltrate the wall of globes.

But they'd been wrong about one thing.

Chen was still there. Chen had been lying in wait. Chen had never ambushed them before. Chen had either been there or not been there. That was all.

An evil star.

Perhaps they should have aborted the mission right then, moved on, found another City, another Company.

viii.
like two people trying
to become one person

Chen ambushed Chen in a corridor distant from their apartment, near the swimming pool. Chen did not reach out to Moss or Grayson, who were already in the apartment; the danger seeped into their minds instead as an unease, took a long time to coalesce. Then burst forth as a star as radiant as Chen's hand drifting bright across the horizon.

It happened too often. This withholding by Chen. This self-sacrifice. They could not tell if this was out of loyalty to his other self, from his pervading guilt, or the simple logic that it made no sense for all three of them to risk harm. Yet each time was more dangerous, for it had come to seem

the Company sensed their presence, their mission, on some subconscious level. Thus cast out all Chens, or, in some cases, killed them, snuffed them out. Or made them more belligerent.

This Chen roared, brought down heavy fists on Chen's back, cursing his own name, as Chen smashed into Chen's midriff, already enraged by his termination.

They remained close as wrestlers, clasping each other's shoulders with meaty hands. The sweat, ache of muscles, and desperation that choreographed their movements. Chen was confident and resigned; he knew from prior experience he likely must fight to the death, as much as he wished not to. Locked now in a fatal embrace, both sets of legs churning, wide stance, looking from above like some bizarre crab or starfish in two parts or like two people trying to merge and become one person.

"Submit," Grayson's Chen muttered in Chen's ear.

"Never. Abomination. Traitor," came the reply.

"Get out. Stop helping them. Stop the hurting."

"Die die die."

Felt the dissolve, fought it, came back into focus.

Chen, between grunts, tried to tear off Chen's left ear with his teeth. So he let his ear fall off, spin across the empty ground, pick itself up, and lurch out of harm's way.

Grayson's Chen knew the panic, understood it: that this Chen could not conceive of the truth but knew another truth. The Company could make people if it wanted, and the thrashing, terrible intensity of attack, the visceral nature of it, meant that Chen, seeing Chen, understood this, too.

All the memories of Chen—of family continents away,

of work history, of hobbies, of relationships—that this was a sham and a shame and that the only way to keep some sense of personhood was to destroy the invader. In some Cities, some Chens might fold under that weight, but most of the time it made the Chens fight long and hard and dirty.

Except Chen didn't care if he was a made thing or not—Moss had cured him of that neurosis—and he had the advantage of having fought Chen before. He knew all of his moves, knew all the ways to end it, including how he had learned to adapt his flesh from Moss, that he could detach his hand and turn it into a dangerous flaming star flying through the sky.

Yet still Chen muttered at Chen as they struggled, pleading with this other self to submit, to give in, that they could work together if only Chen had a chance to explain. Trying again.

"Submit and join us. Two are better than one. What do you owe the Company?"

"Submit and the Company will welcome us back in. Submit and we can both have the life you had before."

"A dead life?"

"*Something to hold on to.*"

But had Chen said that or had Moss's Chen thought it? Who was lying to whom?

As Chen fought back and refused to submit, Grayson's Chen grew weary. Not of the fight, for he had learned to love fighting because at least it ended in a vanquishing that denoted a kind of progress. But as he traded blows with himself—rabbit punches, kicks to the groin—Chen felt something sanded down finally and forever. As his fist struck

Chen's jaw and Chen's fist struck him in the stomach. As they stumbled in the grapple, neither quite going to the ground, Chen realized he was weary of killing himself. He was tired.

This was the fourth time.

With a great spasm and twist of self-loathing, Chen moved to the side and locked his arm around Chen's throat in a choke hold, clambered onto his back, and clasped Chen's torso tight with his legs. Chen fell with Chen on top of him, bucking, trying to get at Chen with elbows, then trying to dislodge Chen's legs.

Chen managed to twist enough to get his fingers under Chen's choke hold and flip so that they were face-to-face on the uneven floor, in the dust and dirt next to the swimming pool. Now each had hands around the other's throat, those bull-like necks, so close they could have kissed or spat or done anything.

Moss had altered Chen's oxygen capacity, or taught him to do so. He never remembered what was augmentation and what was just training. So Chen was content to choke Chen, until Chen passed out and there was a moment when Chen had always, would forever, continue to apply pressure to the throat and Chen would die.

But this Chen, too, must have altered oxygen capacity, or was working from a different equation, and did not tire and did not pass out or die, but only squeezed harder on Chen's neck, too. Which alarmed Chen, and then all the solidarity with his own flesh that he had built up over time . . . gave way.

Grayson's Chen burst at the seams. Became a mound of writhing green salamanders, in a sigh, a deliquescence.

Slipping from Chen's grasp as he gasped and stepped back. In surprise or disgust? For salamander-Chen still formed a rough composite of Chen's form. Slouched over on the ground, the salamanders fierce-eyed, determined to pledge allegiance to an equation made obsolete.

Stared up disoriented at Chen through the array of a thousand eyes and, with a shudder, misdiagnosing, thinking he was back at the wall of globes in the Company building, he screamed. Chen shrieked. The salamanders wailed with him in an uncanny chorus. Even as locked together they clung, embraced, their feet like hooks, a community of flesh desperate not to succumb to a more nomadic impulse. How lonely that would be. For everyone.

Then Grayson was there, enveloping Chen and keeping Chen whole, putting him back together, subsiding the frenzy of the salamanders.

Then Moss was there, subduing the other Chen. Muffling the Chen in waves of green particles, come a little undone herself to undo Chen.

Who, stunned, stumbled now as if through a dream or nightmare. Grappled with this nothing dissipating through the air and made despairing sounds. Subsided, rendered frozen by the pinpricks of Moss's transference of her defensive blood. Moss recoiling at the feel of Chen's blood in contact with her particles.

Grayson found rope in Chen's pack and bound Chen's hands and feet.

"I have you, Chen."

"I have you, Moss."

"Another time, Chen. Another time. But not now."

Chen outside was Chen again. Could not describe the feeling of being so distributed: to have so many bodies at once and so many eyes, and so many beating hearts and breathing lungs. A legion of tiny lives that could not be reduced to equations, that existed in every moment, each unique, nothing about math or structure. He needed music. He needed a huge meal. He would get neither, just the relief of his own labored breathing. Singular.

Charlie X had altered Chen to fail because he was disposable. Moss had made him fail in a way that allowed him to live, that gave some comfort, that was not really failure. That allowed Chen to atone, that manifested in his flesh.

Grayson and Moss looked down at Chen. They could see the imprint of salamander bodies like a fading tattoo. They could see it, so Chen could too. Feel also their concern.

"Should you do it or should I do it?" Grayson asked Chen.

Kill the other Chen.

Chen said, "No! Keep him alive. He might have value."

Chen had never had value because Chen never knew as much as Grayson's Chen. Chen had never suggested saving Chen. It was too dangerous.

Moss put a hand on Chen's shoulder.

"You said the duck is on our side," Chen wheezed out through the retreat of salamanders in his throat. "We can afford to." Just to say something. Just to be normal. Which was impossible.

"The duck was at our side," Moss observed.

True: The duck had appeared next to the swimming pool, watching them. Had it been there the moment before?

Then it was gone again.

The duck had seen Chen explode into salamanders. It had seen Moss help reconstitute Chen.

What else had it seen?

ix.

a creator who no longer remembered the creation

How to explain the weight of the duck with the broken wing? In truth of flesh and blood and light, though it could not fly. The wing deliberate, part of Charlie X's plan, that the duck might always be cast out from the Company. That the duck might register as prey. As low and cast out and as prey.

To the three when they encountered the duck, it was as heavy as if made of brass or steel or gold. The duck's gaze was impervious to the years, pinned them down with that weight. Always when they arrived: that urgent, nagging question. Is the duck with us or against us? Does the duck recognize us?

The duck represented a paradox. It roamed where it would, and wherever it patrolled for the Company it also negated anywhere within its shadow the Company's surveillance. The duck could do that, to lesser and greater degrees, across all of the Cities.

"Schrödinger's duck."

"Heidegger's duck."

"Swedenborg's duck."

"Seneca's duck."

Charlie X's duck.

The worst versions of the duck: Carnivorous, enflamed, the cruel lizardous eye. Oozing a thin crust of blood that dried on the mottled white. Oracular stigmata, appraising. Price of seeing too much of the future. Most often observed replicating the murders of birds of prey—bill sharp, serrated in microscopic detail. Buried in a limp rat-thing, tearing out the guts. Gulping them down like a ghoulish stork. Gnawing on what was left in an artistic way, the delicacy in how long the duck could leave the recipient of its attentions alive.

It would look up from feasting with a mechanical grace and hunger, as if lusting for meat in a way that festered. Fostered the impression screams were more important than hunger.

Once, twice, the three witnessed the duck eviscerating a fox it had pinned to the sand, from back legs to snout, with the spurs on its scaly feet. And then the duck did bring down its head like a hammer that became an ice pick that split the fox's head in a crack and splatter of blood and brain matter. A sound that carried over the sands.

But the duck ate no part of either fox. Perhaps wary of

a trap. That the foxes might come free from the inside out, might somehow conquer it postmortem. That the foxes still spoke to one another when dead, voices floating in the air, seemed a desecration by the duck, but Moss could not be sure. All that seemed sure is that Charlie X hated the foxes. Or had once hated one fox.

Of the broken wing, the best that could be said is that the wing left a smile upon many a neck and torso. But never on a face. For the creature could in a motion reminiscent of some awkward bat unfold and unfurl and extend.

The wing by will locked in place. The edge knife-sharp and serrated. It with willful industry and psychotic intent vivisected and hacked apart scavengers as large as men and larger. With a zigzagging approach once taught perhaps but now as automatic as a stitched pattern.

Then came the sliding in a wet and separated slump to the dust, the dirt, the scavenger forever caught in a bloodstained, anguished look of confusion at the method of its own ending. Until the sun and smaller scavengers still did their work and turned the anguish into a smile. Because dead things felt only love for the universe.

Sometimes, the duck would distract with the voice of your beloved dead, plucked from your mind, and then dig into your brain like a worm or grub, and try to live in there for a while, eating out your thoughts until you were a husk that twitched and slobbered and spasmed in the sand. At which point, reduced to harmlessness, the duck would stab you with its beak wherever best to place a spigot. Bleed you out while eating you alive.

There came then, Moss knew, in some victims, the heights of ecstatic experience. A lightness that carried the mind off into the clouds to look down on the twisting and shaking mess of carcass without worry or care. Despite the pain that had arrived before that moment.

Oh happy memory for Charlie X, who had no memories anymore. Oh, happy days of youth evoked by the duck. The one he'd nursed back to health. The one he'd been given as a gift. The one he'd rescued from a zoo. The one he'd kidnapped at a park. Depending on Charlie X's mood, the story changed, on a sliding scale of the sentimental that Chen could map to the cruel.

The one he'd told Chen about even as he created the demonic version, no space between the molecules of air that shouted *Lie!* and those that flowed from his mouth to tell what he thought was the truth, in that moment.

Who knew what was truth and what was story?

The logical next question, more remote because the answer was usually the same: *Where is Charlie X now?* Nowhere. Nowhere. Dead. Forgotten. Rags buried in sand, buried in the past. Just the duck left behind.

But that was not the case in this City.

Charlie X, a ghost given flesh, rising up impossible to meet them across the years. Yet they could not meet him. Must not risk that in his disturbed mind might still exist a memory of Chen, of Moss and the wall of globes inside the Company. And, so, seeing Charlie X from afar as they had headed for the Balcony Cliffs, by the polluted river . . . the

three let him pass unhindered. Did not call out. Did not admit to the past. Hardly discussed it after.

They'd never turned him to their cause, either too broken or not broken enough. But here, and most places now, he had already long past been abandoned or been kicked out by the Company. Unable to use the micro-tears created by the portals that allowed Moss a way to come through. Burdened by the bat-like hardening of features that the Company had imposed on him. That never truly fit. That proclaimed mask or helmet or cage. And how he breathed uneven through it, rasping, and how the mice living in his throat bulged there, clung to soft tissue with their sanitized toes. How long it had taken Charlie X not to claw at his throat, for all that lived inside it? Knew, somewhere deep inside, that he always went mad, went bad, could not be trusted, lived in a place where the landscape had been stripped bare.

Yet still, sometimes, in some scenarios, Chen would pause in the shadow of some version of a ruined building as some version of Charlie X stumbled by. As some version of Charlie X cowered in an empty cistern. Or lay quiet under a trapdoor to catch his prey. Or sat in the dust and wept in a self-pity that Moss found intolerable.

"Should we end him?"

A pause.

"No." This from Grayson. Always.

It would be for themselves, not for him. He could do no harm now that he had not already achieved. In the grand scheme, to the three he had truly become a ghost. What could they say but words over his grave as he walked away from them, mumbling to himself.

Besides, Grayson argued, there was the risk: They did not know what Charlie X's death might mean to the duck.

Dark bird. Dark secret. They knew not what it hid, what was artifice and what was content. Peel away that layer, find a deeper monster still.

What did Charlie X scrawl in the sand with a stick? A design, a half-remembered purpose that they recognized because it was still, in part, their own. And, looking back when well south of him, through the binoculars, the wistful way the duck with the broken wing had halted in shadowing the three.

Out there on the broken plain, they could not encounter one another. Either the Company or Charlie X, in his last days before being cast out, had intervened, that neither should hurt the other nor acknowledge the other. Nor see the other. And if it should look like their paths might intersect, one or the other would step to the side and not know why, but continue on then, fellow ghosts ghosting straight through to the other side.

A creator who no longer remembered the creation: Wasn't that one definition of a god?

For each circling lunge, the duck had an answer and soon enough Charlie X had whipped up a cloud of dust in his exertions and his foul cursing, and when the dust settled, the duck had disappeared once more.

Escaped to shadow the three, made up ground in an uncanny way, as if when they looked back to chart its progress, the duck occurred in the City via time-lapse photography,

so that it always resided several yards in advance of where it should have been.

Moss was a heretic. Moss sometimes thought that Charlie X had, in a way, brought them together. That somehow, with the duck as the fulcrum, Charlie X had unwittingly orchestrated their resistance prior to crumbling before the onslaught of his own trauma.

Yet perhaps Moss had the right to think this way. For Charlie X had created her.

x.
a shadow
of a vastness

That night, while Grayson slept and Chen recovered, Moss dimmed her thoughts from them, crept through their defenses, snuck out of the Balcony Cliffs. Chen and Grayson never really slept. Perhaps because they were too connected or just couldn't pretend anymore. But she hoped they slept in some sense, that what she did now was muted to them.

Chen had kept arguing that he should be the one for this mission, that he could convince the fish to help them. But Moss had decided she couldn't let him. Wasn't as suited for it, taxed and tested by the other Chen, and having only his

blunt, Company ways to complete the mission; just wanted to spare her being hurt.

Still, Grayson would never understand. Not the risk. Not the trade Moss might have to make. The decision she had come to.

So she followed the ravine, the trace of water down the center. In a trance. In a kind of ebb and flow as she abandoned human form. A carpet of moss roiling across the dirt, sand, and rocks. A screed that rewrote whatever it encountered, so the dirt had new properties and the sand burgeoned with new life and the rocks began processes that might not germinate for centuries.

An onslaught, a hidden invasion. Runneling like an unseen, weightless, slow-motion avalanche, her advance guard become her rearguard. Spreading out to the sides and then in again. Folding over and over.

Lingering in the roots of shattered trees and the neural networks of fungi. All of it battered, not at capacity but alive still. A shadow of a vastness. And she existed there, splayed out across those axes in a special kind of ecstasy. Remembered the other ways. Thought, perhaps, to close down human-type thoughts, to stay. To exist just in that moment and the next. To not go back or go forward.

Exhausting. It exhausted to be so close to Grayson, to Chen. Ecstatic. Amazing, that intimacy. To lie down upon a bed with two others enfolded there, not cheek to cheek but the same cheek as one. Yes, ecstatic, but exhausting, exhausting, exhausting. Never alone, and Moss herself so many Mosses and thus never alone in herself either.

Moss kept the human form for certain advantages, to live with Grayson and Chen. Because it helped Chen hold his body together. She did it for other people.

Become nothing or everything. Nothing that could be other than nothing. Nothing that could feel what Moss had felt at the hands of Charlie X.

To be something again in the end—something that would mean everything to Grayson. That was the price, the price, the price. And at the very end, to come back into the consciousness that human recognized as human, that she might parlay with the fish on their behalf.

At the bottom of the ravine, the blue fox waited, as she had known he would. And by that sign Moss knew she hadn't slipped into another place, another time. For this would never happen again and had never happened before.

"Are you ready?" the blue fox asked.

"Yes," she said.

No, she wasn't ready, she'd never be ready. Ready would be too late.

Or so the fox had convinced her.

xi.
such savage mockery
of the tidal pools

In some Cities, the leviathan of the holding ponds had suffered at the Company's hands. Open sores. Burns. In those places, Moss would sing to the leviathan to soothe it and dull its pain receptors and show it images of a limitless and fecund sea. Once, all she could do was ease the creature toward a merciful death.

Do you see me? Here I am.

Casting out a line before ever she saw the beast.

Here, the leviathan had been smarter, luckier, more dangerous, adapted, been deemed useless by the Company. In truth the leviathan, pure, was natural to this place. Had

not been created but had lived here all its preternaturally long life.

I am not a threat. Not a threat. Not a threat.

In this version of the City, the leviathan was almost one hundred years old. Called it Botch, after a long-dead painter. But it wasn't Botched. That was just a personal lexicon, the dark humor of reluctant soldiers. In which they sometimes called the blue fox Flue or Flu or even Flow. As a contagion that spread among the foxes and perhaps others.

I am here to parlay. This is parlay. I will send you what parlay means.

Botch, Fish, Leviathan had one massive dead white eye that was always weeping salt. "Grayson's fish," Chen joked, gently.

Ancient and weathered and huge, and even then the veteran of a hundred battles. Had devoured so many Company rejects and regrets, even though itself rejected.

Your enemies are our enemies.

A lyrical music that came out of its ugly grouper-esque mouth. That at a low lull could mesmerize prey out across the water to drown in its maw. That, brought from beautiful to a sawlike piercing, could stun at close range. A defiantly ugly fish wandering between the size of rhinoceros and whale.

A ripe stench that would've wrinkled Grayson's nostrils, sent a wince across her face. As if Botch brought with it an olfactory record of every chemical, kind of offal, algae, muck it had passed through.

Botch had formidable defenses. Gills that pivoted outward sudden into blades. Razor scales that could angle at

signs of danger and gouge at the touch. The mighty jaws lined with diseased and glistening yellow teeth that spread illness as well as lacerations. Strong wide fins meant for both walking and swimming. If it ever made it to an ocean, the leviathan would grow and grow and become a despotic lord among fish. Freshwater or salt? It had a map in its head that yearned for any kind of water.

Things I can give you in exchange . . .

Botch, wallowing in the sucking mud of a bog-like pond tempered by patches of yellowing grasses. Such a savage mockery of her tidal pools. The dash-dots of flies skimming over meant as cameras once but now click-clicked more out of ritual than purpose.

Botch wallowing and Moss letting herself go wide and shallow to cover the mud pond in a sheen of tiny green-and-white flowers lashed together like chain mail, from which something vaguely like a face held court and hailed Botch as friend.

In the moonlight and the shadow, which neither registered, given excellent night vision.

Botch caught in some dreaming pattern as it gulped down a cache of screaming alcohol minnows.

A kind of response, interpreted in the flush of first contact as: <<*You think you are everything, everywhere. You think that the world is not everything, everywhere, around you.*>>

The coordinates of control for a dreadnought like Botch were so different than for Moss. They spoke not

in fish nor in the language of moss. Because they were neither fish nor moss. Not in person-speech. Because they were not human.

But not in something newly made or ordered. Not machine language or codes or mazes. It had to be translated on either side, strained through layers, halting, pushing forward. Sometimes what translated into supposed words was emotion or reaction. Approximates that had to be trusted in the moment, before these approximates became slippery and escaped into the mire. Because the translation was a kind of virus, and Moss trusted she was infecting the fish and not the fish Moss.

<<*What can this be seen as but attack?*>> Botch didn't say, would never say, and yet, in some sense, did say . . . but remained there in front of her. The stillness of Botch, staring out across the floating field of Moss-blossoms was her clue that he wanted to eat her. If only he could find a heart to rip out and devour among all those flowers.

This beast that could carry her, some part of her, some version. Could find a way or buy them more time, or times, of a sort. Not the mission as agreed to by Grayson or Chen. But what she had worked through with the fox. A way that appealed to the plant cells in her, the moss and the lichen. If nothing else.

She told Botch that she truly saw him. That she could trace Botch back through the outline of his scars. For there was not a part of Botch's body that did not have scars and so he was now white as snow, white as preternatural, white as something that did not belong in the City. White had not the strength of stone nor the armor of death, of

fossil. But was only weakness revealed, the language of the future.

Unwound each scar from Botch's body, each as it had happened, and she told Botch, who had forgotten, what each scar meant, and how it had happened and why and what else had been in the world around Botch at the time. Each scar removed in this way that told the story of Botch's long life, and with each story Botch *gained* with the loss, and at the end, bereft of scars and thus of wounds, stood before Moss shining with an original truth.

For an instant, Botch was new again and the eye was bright but the murder had left it.

I need something from you. Something important.

It was not a thing she could force, but Moss tired of force and felt diminished by force and wanted as little of that poison in her as she could manage.

Part of me will protect a part of you. I will protect you forever and a day as I am able. I will be a type of armor.

For no one had ever gleaned that such a monster might feel the need for protection. Somewhere deep down in the depths of it, in the sunless ocean within.

<<I don't know you. You know me and now I remember me. But I don't know you.>>

But it wasn't said. It wasn't bellowed or sung. Yet Moss knew.

This is me.

This is me.

You are me.

Who are me? But she knew who are me. She knew. Down in the burning shed of her soul.

And let Botch in, even as Botch exploded through the mud, dove deep into the dark water, Moss leaping upon his back, dragged under, pulled below, breathing, not breathing, torn asunder, clinging in all the ways moss could cling, to the back of the beast that meant to kill her.

xii.

to be both receiver and received

Moss against Moss, when it happened, rare, was like intricate garden combat. Between plants. Between obstinate weeds. Pugnacious. Sped up, slowed down. First one in retreat across a dusty yard full of skeletons and then the other. Add a third, a fourth Moss, drawn to the same reality, and there was in the confluence, the flux of outspread filaments and curling grasp nothing but the bliss of tiny flowers and exploding spores.

Until, finally, there was no difference between attacker and attacked, and no shame in cease-fire, because Moss could not tell herself from her self. From that place of comfort, the comfort of being greater than before, Moss

could rise again in human form. One Moss. Ever divisible. Under no god. Under no rules of ungoverned, forgotten countries.

Many times—not this time, when Moss had stolen out to parlay with a fish—the mission meant Moss consolidated would stand leaking green mist out of the helmet of her contamination suit, as the three lurked in the shelter of the ravine. Leaking in loops and spirals that settled thick to the ground, began to form a hazy emerald specter that resembled Moss. When Moss closed her suit, it was done. There, before them, would stand what appeared to be another Moss, fuzzy at the edges, but the same warm smile. The same inquisitive look.

A gaze that transmitted light from one semblance of an eye to another. All of Moss was eyes. None of Moss was eyes.

Moss would talk to her doppelgänger and her doppelgänger would set off on the mission, accompanied by Chen, who could navigate the wasteland to the holding ponds and who turned on camouflage so, in his suit, he could not be seen except by arcane means. While Moss's doppelgänger, this pointillist portrait of her, disassembled and reassembled by Chen's side, in a shimmer of molecules that leapt out across the sky, circled back, formed a film creeping fast forward across the ground. Chen would wait at the holding ponds, while the wraith of Moss-like would spiral past and visible-invisible to the Company sensors, penetrate the Company building and complete Moss's mission for her.

Or that had been the plan. In the past.

It wasn't safe for Moss to get closer, for Moss was the way

out. Without Moss, they'd never make it to another City if they failed.

Moss did not just tend tidal pools. Often, before Grayson, Moss sent ripples across those still surfaces. About the creatures who lived there and what their lives were like. She looked up from the pools, become what lived there, staring as the giant looming down to peer in, to be both receiver and received. In an endless amplified loop. Slipped across realities. Very tactical, as Grayson had said, and yet infinite. Each time it changed them, just a little. But Moss couldn't remember what they might have been before, at the start. None of them could.

Moss couldn't extend the field. But, at a price, she could become a door—they walked through her and she followed, and wasn't that the definition of sacrifice?

As much as clinging in a film of green to the back of Botch as he dove so far and so deep, and twisted and bucked to dislodge what could not be dislodged, for Moss's grip extended beneath Botch's scarred skin, hooks in deep. Even as bits of her tore away from the violence of Botch's panicked tunneling into the depths. Into the darkness.

But she could see what lay there. The skeletons in a familiar tableau. The memories she should not have. Made manifest by the nature of the mission, the nature of her body.

Hush now, hush now.

Soon you will be free. I will make you free.

But could Moss make her free? Could she free them both?

No, but I can . . .

This was the part where things began to fall apart, because they were meant to fall apart, because they were meant to fall apart because they meant to fall apart. The ways they'd been cut off. How Moss had not yet shared that she could reach one more City, and maybe one more after that, if lucky. But the respite the three had always had before, retreat to the tidal pools of the coast for a time . . . that was closed to them now.

The Company had snuffed out the gaps. Redrawn the map, smaller and smaller. The end would come soon. And, too, because Chen was falling apart and though Moss could hold him together, against Charlie X's curse, that, too, would come to pass, inevitable.

There was no path by which she could un-curse a genetic code so intimately tied to breath.

Nor could she deny what the fox had told her, what had finally decided her. They were running out of Cities, of Companies. Realities were finite. The fox had found their limit out on the edge of beyond, had let her into his mind enough to see. Slivers that ended with seven. All the slivers you could want, that math could provide, but only up to seven. And perhaps seven brave acts were necessary, too. Not just three. Infiltration from the sky, yes, but from the very rotting bones of the land. The carcass of a behemoth falling apart, rising up to meet the rain.

Reaching the outermost point, or at least the farthest that could be borne. In a suit, looking at rock, rock underfoot. Unsure if the formation was the suggestion of a helmet, of a face. Or just a coincidence, an outline that meant nothing.

Would never know.

But Moss knew.

Botch stopped writhing and twisting, settled unsettled deeper in the mud. But still she could not relax. There were things to plant in Botch's brain and body that would feel for a time like worms eating flesh but were only Moss's map. Were only a version of Moss.

You do not need to pretend with me.

Direct, into Botch's brain. She could see into there, knew Botch pretended dumb animal but was not really that either.

A kind of shuddering shrug from the fish.

<<Danger. Too dangerous.>>

Moss projected a scene in Botch's head. Just Botch wandering between the holding ponds. Just old reliable Botch, looking for food. Gobbling up misshapen mudpuppies and toads and worms and fellow fish. Just happy to come closer and closer to the Company. And who would really be able to tell the sheen of green atop Botch's scales? A coat of algae picked up in some other pond. That sweet-sharp smell that wasn't meant but similar. Should Botch smell good? And then the green mostly gone and Botch long since well away from danger.

<<Why should I?>>

To live. To thrive. To continue to rule over all of this. Botch could not botch that habitat more than the Company. It was contaminated, wild, always polluted but always resisting. Botch would grow huge and rule over all, a benevolent tyrant, and if, in the process, the Company—contaminated across all the versions—fell away, then maybe the foxes would dance across the floor of the dead Company building, but they would never have a use for the holding ponds.

Best you be ruled by your own.

<<I rule already.>>

Yet there came the nod in her mind that told her Botch would not fight them. That Botch feared the unknown watchful preternatural nature of Moss more than the known cruelty of the Company. Mistrusted her less.

Botch let Moss in and they were both by the sea, by Moss's tidal pools. Under the ruined arches. Botch was small again, Botch was so very small smooth still in a tidal pool and Moss, giant, peered into that pool and shone down like the sun on Botch. Covering Botch. Beaming love down on Botch in rays of calm.

Botch's one eye milky and closed. Opened. Moss knew now that Botch had been born that way. Knew that the eye saw more than the other one. Knew Botch would not remember their parlay because she would give him the mercy of forgetting something so human. Give herself that mercy.

<<I dream of fresh, open water. I dream of sunlight and cool mud. I dream of the food walking ecstatic, into my open mouth.>>

Was that Moss or Botch? For some part of Botch would forever be with Moss now. Part of Moss would, clandestine, contaminate all the tidal pools. If they were lucky.

Botch was very large, towering over her reflection in the glimmering water, and she was small and tired.

Goodbye, Moss said to her doppelgänger or her doppelgänger said to her. *Goodbye and hello.*

The body did not exist separate from the soul because the soul didn't exist. But the future never left the past behind, either.

Her doppelgänger peered out from a burning shed and said nothing more. Shut the door, with her self inside. Taken by the conflagration. Burning at the heart of Botch.

The duck with the broken wing had not appeared during their parlay; the duck was nowhere nearby. Relief beneath the weariness of what she'd lost to Botch. What she'd conceded to the fox. But she never thought about why, until later.

That perhaps the duck had already been there.

xiii.
disposable and finite and vulnerable

There wasn't always *mission* for the three. You couldn't mission forever, Moss would say, or there would be no mission. Building an image from before as prod and tease: When she had hopped between the tidal pools and had run onto the beach just to pretend she had legs, to pretend she was not a wall of onrushing onrushing wall onrushing.

Danced on the beach, all alone. Had made play into a game of tag that wanted to be caught, to be it. Nothing must be glum. Nothing must be serious, even if it was serious. Not all the time.

"This is what we would look like as fish." (Chen's idea,

laughing as he said it, but Moss had nodded serious, still recovering from her mission. "I would bob near the surface, Grayson would be some kind of barracuda, and Moss would be a school of minnows hiding in seaweed.")

People were serious, but the world wasn't serious. Not the drunk, lurching beetle that had feasted on the remains of an alcohol minnow. Not the seaweed that brilliant and wet-slapped displayed its color and its texture there, against the silly sea anemones blazing forth their tentacles. And if there were fewer creatures on this Earth man had made, then still they took time to be still. To be thoughtful. To frolic. Before returning to the eat, drink, forage world.

The three played cards sometimes to take the edge off. They had an old battered deck. Or played catch with a worn tennis ball.

Or, as here, as now, standing outside the south entrance of the Balcony Cliffs, each aware of the slant of ravine and half-dead trees through which they could still see the Company, for purest white did blaze.

Grayson's eagle eye trained on the holding ponds, that she might determine from some break in routine or intervention if the Company had sussed Moss's secret meeting the night before.

Moss: "Never liked team sports, though."

Grayson, affectionate: "You are a team sport."

Chen found this so funny he could not stop laughing. It cut through his disapproval of Moss sneaking off, which evaporated as he would too, one day.

They had been in this spot before. Sometimes this was where they found the dollhouse, half-crushed, the one they

used to strategize, and brought it back inside, repaired it. Best they could.

This time they had found what Grayson called a Frisbee.

"What's a phriz bee?" Moss asked.

"This."

"This plastic disk."

"And you throw it."

"Why?"

"For fun."

"Team sport."

Grayson zipped the Frisbee to Moss, who threw it straight up in the air like it was made of heat.

Yet somehow it came down and leveled out and sped right into Chen's hand. He liked the grooved feel of it, yet the smoothness. His hand was always cataloging new textures. He kept squares of linen paper to write on, for the lines across it that felt like connection, like it had already been written on.

They backed up into a proper triangle.

Chen threw the Frisbee to Grayson, who caught it, held it a moment, tried not to laugh at the quizzical, worried look on Moss's face.

"They really did have teams," Grayson said.

"When?"

"Ages ago. Long ago. I don't remember when." It was too painful to think of her childhood, because she could remember when none of this could be thought of as real.

Chen thought he could remember when, too, but how could he be sure?

"What else like this did they have?" Moss asked.

Grayson ignored her, ambushed her instead with "Why did you go off on your own? Why didn't you let us go with?" Deft like that—wanting to come at Moss sideways. But Moss knew it was just a reminder not to do it again, ignored her.

Grayson sailed the Frisbee Moss's way, but too high, but then Moss was too high, and smoldering green in a way that made Grayson lustful and in awe, and the Frisbee was caught, but not in the normal way—as if bouncing off a wall that fell away in the next moment, and there was an explosion of mint scent and the Frisbee, which had flickered out, appeared in Chen's outstretched hand so quick he dropped it and, cursing, retrieved it from the ground.

Then he froze.

"How do we know it's the same Frisbee?"

They couldn't, Grayson knew.

"Are we playing Frisbee in another place too?"

Grayson leapt as she caught the Frisbee from Chen.

"No," Moss said. "Somewhere else we kick a ball with our feet."

"We already did that," Grayson said, passing the Frisbee back to Chen, Chen back to Grayson. "Remember? Many Companies ago."

"They do that now in the City. This City," Moss said. "Give me the Frisbee."

Grayson and Chen both chuckled. "No," they said, and moved so Moss was between them.

"But not in teams—kicking the ball," Chen said.

The Frisbee passing around Moss, tricking Moss, or she was letting herself be tricked, as she leapt for it but they were swift too and Chen had his hand tricks and looked her off,

made her grow tall in the wrong direction, then ducked under and around.

"Give me the Frisbee!" Moss shouted.

"You'll just do something weird with it," Grayson said.

"But you love that."

It was true. Grayson did love that. But they had a sweat on. They were competitive, Grayson and Chen both, in a way Moss was not. She was competitive, but not in the singular.

So they kept it away from Moss for a while and then she tired of their trickery.

Moss became a wall between them and intercepted the Frisbee. It went from Chen through Moss and out the other side came thrown at Grayson a ball the size of her head instead and Grayson ducked and fell and Moss, again herself, whatever that meant, laughed in the liquid, vegetal way she had and Chen smiled and radiated his love to them both while Grayson feigned outrage.

"You've changed the future," Chen said, to change the subject, just in case. "I can feel it. We can go home now."

Moss and Grayson just stared at Chen.

Which home?

The Frisbee did not return and they did not return to the Frisbee. Inside the Balcony Cliffs, they sprawled across the same worn bed. Falling into another type of exploration and of play. The sense of completeness that was being overwhelmed, of being held tight and surrounded by Moss. Of how Chen rose like a mountain no matter what he did. How Grayson's sharpness reduced under her clothes to a softness,

a vulnerability, and she allowed herself to relax in their embrace.

"What would you have done if not for this?" Moss asked Grayson. If the Earth had not been so wounded. If the Company hadn't destroyed so much.

"I would have come searching for you at the tidal pools."

"No, you wouldn't. You wouldn't know to. You wouldn't know me. You wouldn't stumble on me by chance."

"Somehow, I would have."

The three knew they were disposable and finite and vulnerable. But they also knew they were rare and precious. Had never appeared at the outskirts of the City and strode across the desert sands to meet their doubles, stare into their eyes as if into a mirror, and see, naked there, a similar intent.

"And you, Moss?" asked Chen.

"I would have lived out my days by the sea. I would have been alone in my thoughts. I would have cut myself off from everyone or anyone."

Grayson was glad, for she knew that if she ever died, Moss might go back to her tidal pools.

"And you, Chen?" Grayson asked.

"It doesn't matter what I would have done. Only what I did," Chen said. But they knew he didn't mean it, just that Chen did not want to have a future that did not include Grayson, Moss, their purpose.

Limbs that couldn't be separated, didn't want to be separated, were not always human but more right because of it. How Moss's kisses came from everywhere. How Chen became so giddy and silly. How Grayson's urgency became their urgency. Held by so many and so much and never

being alone, separate again, and the loss in the withdrawal of the tide, and how they would long for the next time, and how it made a mockery of the communion mind-to-mind that they always shared. How you could never trade the physical for the intimacy of thought. How this might be the last time.

Moss would tell them in the morning, would explain in the morning. As they stood outside, looking down at the Company building.

Maybe they would understand.

Somewhere, in another City, a Frisbee had clattered on rock, come to soft scrunch on sand. Somewhere, a child's ball, kicked, had disappeared in midair.

The child changed forever. Believing in spirits or miracles or in loss or transformation. Or maybe believing in nothing at all.

Then the door closed and Moss was just in one place, one time, again. Sprawled there on the bed.

Rebel and traitor both.

xiv.
the sickness found
in the midst of beauty

What had Chen done for the Company? Before he betrayed the Company? Before he stole Charlie X's journal and sent it and the salamander through the wall of globes to another place?

Chen-conscripted disposed of dying biotech at the holding ponds. Chen-volunteer checked the Company's products for signs of illness, so that the sick could be sent to the holding ponds. Or given over to Charlie X.

Conscripted or volunteer, Chen told himself that he worked hard for an absent family, a wife, two children, and a grandmother that Grayson's Chen had come to think of

as far-distant stars, as remote as anything in the night sky. Perhaps corrupted by the idea that they didn't really exist, had never really existed. But also because Chen-now knew it didn't matter: He would never see them again; they lay so many realities behind and whatever copies lived here belonged to the Chen they had imprisoned. The one that periodically used it for freedom.

Chen-that-was lived in his Balcony Cliffs apartment and came to the Company to work weeklong shifts, sleeping in a cubicle bed among the others. All day long, Chen mostly saw the biotech. Shoveled it into the holding ponds, to be preyed upon—floating, struggling, drowning—by the creatures that already lived there, that had refused to die as predicted or desired. Good, the Company said. They can serve a purpose. And so they did.

The people Chen worked with faded and shrank into a landscape of slow-moving shadows in his mind. The globes they worked with a form of contamination, like radiation and mercury poisoning, but different because biological and temporal.

Chen wore special clothing to protect him from the wall of globes when he worked there. Localized fields leading to other places once the "product" was complete. Areas of temporal contamination near the Company building. Most of the time, it just made people sick. Sometimes it corrupted the body in a way that the body became unstable, could not decide whether to live here or there, then or now.

There was only Charlie X's voice, coming through from the secret room on the other side of the wall of globes, the side Chen wasn't allowed to see. The place where Charlie X

kept his journal. Except, if you looked at the reflections in the globes . . . you could see the distorted face of Charlie X. See the journal, on the corner of the desk. How often Charlie X referred to it. How he depended on it. Perhaps, too, the green tracery that was evidence of Moss, but how was Chen to have read that? There, so close to Moss, never knowing Moss. Not then. (Or as Chen clarified, "A Chen knew about a Moss." Somewhere/when. "Just not me.")

But Moss did exist there, on the other side. But Moss did see Chen, observed Chen. Knew Chen's equations helped stabilize and rationalize horrors. That Chen's equations even rationalized horrors Charlie X perpetrated upon her. In the way mosses experience the world, could "see" or "hear" or "know."

So, in time, Moss knew that there were Chens who could not cope with what they had been asked to do, when Grayson asked her for conscripts or volunteers who might help their cause.

People who might turn into monsters briefly, but must become human again, no matter what the cost.

What was a person but someone who turned monstrous, anyway? What was a person, in Moss's experience, but a kind of demon.

Chen, volunteer, donned the gloves and special clothes to inspect the biotech contained in the wall of globes. The wall was where he spent most of his time. The wall was what, in the end, broke Grayson's Chen. Broke more than him. And why not? There was no weakness in that. You looked into a

face unlike yours that was still too familiar. A face destined for and destroyed by servitude or entertainment at best, and might now serve a lower task still: As protein for some other creature made for servitude or entertainment that had failed the test and waited in the holding ponds.

At one point, indoctrinated, it must have seemed a good job, a noble task. Something beautiful to take such raw material and make it purposeful. But this faded soon enough.

Chen learned to recognize the glint behind the dull sheen of eyes: the understanding and resentment that fate, that chance, had placed their particular form of consciousness in such a context.

Whether housed in the brilliant red-and-white spines of an animal like a lionfish but made to walk on land, lemur eyes staring from the body of a coiled green lizard, or the amorphous quiver of a converted sea anemone strobing green and purple.

How did any Chen endure it past the first days to pass the boundary of a week, a month, one year, five years. To don the gloves, to push hands through the viscous membrane of a particular globe lodged in the wall, to palpitate and push, to knead, and to judge while applying the sensors. Perhaps to find the false richness of sickness, which so often manifested as a brightness or even, initially, an augmented talent, an intelligence beyond the required parameters or a skill that had never been intended for this particular product.

Some pretended sickness, the more clever of the animals, and he had learned over time that cleverness existed as much among those with inhuman faces as those with bodies that in some manner mimicked the human. For

even embedded within that wall like bizarre floating jewels, some of those he inspected must have heard the myths surrounding the holding ponds. That if you made it to the holding ponds, you might die brutally and of the instant, but also that you might become free, or have a chance at freedom.

But it was the one that spoke to Chen that took him finally, even though once he no longer lived within a space that the Company might approve of, once he had moved past the point on the map where he might still know where he was . . . he knew that it should have come earlier, at any other time, on any other subject.

The agony that was the speech, a human attribute issuing forth from a nonhuman mouth, that he responded to, that had value to him. Or woke him from a trance, from a state of being asleep while standing, while going about the rituals of his day.

The way it was said to Chen, as he had one glove through the membrane and was holding the creature, which presented as a thistle-bright hedgehog face erupting from something with too many legs, all of it bathed in plush golden fur. Holding it in such a way that he could have crushed it as the creature spoke, so that he did not have to hear that voice. A brave voice, a voice that sounded like no other because this creature had never existed before and so he could not describe the voice to another person. Except to say it was like the thrushing of a beating of soft wings that had been doused in calm waters.

After, Chen had stumbled out of the Company building, walked past the holding ponds, staggered lost and bereft

across the sand, first to the wooded ravine and then to a southern entrance of the Balcony Cliffs. But he could not enter, as if a wall of force held him in check, as if there were a physical barrier, but it was just the trauma in his mind. He stopped, bent over, breathing heavily, outside the Balcony Cliffs. He knelt in the gravel, staring unfocused back at the distant Company building.

It was there that Moss and Grayson found him. Eventually. In time. The Chen they needed. The Chen who knew the Company. The Chen who knew the wall of globes and their terrible cargo.

But Chen never told them what the thistle-bright hedgehog creature had said to him. There, in the globe, as it died in his hands from whatever had been done to it on the other side of the wall, what it could not recover from. What Chen could not recover from.

His nightmares he would never burden Grayson and Moss with. But in Chen's dreams the ceiling of the Company building fell away and the globes in the wall floated off into the night sky, leaving behind the Company and all categories of hurt, of injury.

Sometimes, Chen confessed to Moss, he followed them, floated off into the heavens and never came back. And when this happened in the dream, Chen wept, for he had a sense of contentment such as he had never experienced before.

But in truth, their Chen had walked back into the Company building, had worked there for months more before leaving. Waiting for the moment. Sabotaging what he could.

Saw the salamander, large and constrained, curled in the globe. The piercing way it looked at him, the autonomy

there, and knew he could not fail that gaze a second time. Not and live.

If the hedgehog creature broke Chen, perhaps the salamander saved him. Or, at least, that was how Chen's equations told the story. Part of the story.

And so Chen had sent the salamander through the wall of globes into another world. One where the Company had a foothold, but hadn't conquered yet. Where the salamander might have a chance.

And, in a moment of opportunity, sent Charlie X's precious journal after, tumbling down, there one moment.

Gone the next.

XV.

there was no path out
no escape

Then, it was too late. Now, it was too late.

The morning of the next day, as they stood outside the Balcony Cliffs, ready for the next phase. The duck risen up before them as a storm. Vast and dark and deranged: An apparition that dried up the air around it, burned the oxygen so that they were gasping for breath outside the door leading into the Balcony Cliffs. An apparition that blotted out the sky and singed their skin, scalded their senses so they did not want to see or hear or smell or taste or feel. Made the air thick with red dust and dried blood and tiny flaps of metal that cut their faces.

The darkness beneath the duck, sensed by Moss, had

escaped, or been let loose or deployed for the first time. It welled up, oozed, and rose, to spread across the horizon and within their minds as a high, black wall. The scrabbling, terrible presence, demanding to be let in. Knew, three as one, that once it locked into place, they would be lost. *You are broken; let me fix you.*

Moss could feel it. An enclosure. A capture or containment, her doppelgänger locked in place. A sensation that made her gasp.

The past always waited. To wound, to rend, to tear.

"My double is compromised," she said to Chen, to Grayson.

Grayson staring at her sharp with that all-revealing eye. "Your double?"

Her doppelgänger was in the prison that was Botch. No longer in control. Small in the tidal pools. Useless. Nothing they did from afar could help. Nothing from close by. Yet she could sense particles of her other self in the air around them, in the dissipated image of the duck. What did this mean?

The southern door would not open. Chen put his shoulder against it. Moss pried at the seams. Grayson faced the storm, gun drawn, feeling helpless. There was no path out, no escape.

The shape rammed into the Balcony Cliffs, lost its form, became a chaos of loose particles in the air and the wind shoving and smashing into them. In the high keening they heard the sound of part of the ruined roof coming free and walls creaking with the stress, trying to withstand what could not be withstood.

The scrabbling, terrible presence, demanding to be let in. Knew, three as one, that once it locked in place, once it splintered their skulls, broke into their minds, they would be lost.

Rocks and branches smashed against the wall around them.

But still the southern door would not open.

"Stand aside," Grayson shouted.

She shot, four times. The bullets wedged in the metal. But the door would not open.

"Moss should take us out of here!" Chen shouted.

"I can't. The storm's in the way," Moss shouted back.

The storm didn't just exist in this space, in this time. It was obscuring her internal map, her compass. It was muffling the information, closing down the escape routes. Particles of her other self used to confuse her uncanny senses.

The door snapped open from the inside and Chen raged out. Glistening in that dark light, possessed by a terrible spirit, a terrible impulse. Shining like a beacon of burning white light. Face torn apart by rictus. Eyes turned up in his head.

Nocturnalia.

Moss understood: The duck had turned him. Some part of Charlie X had turned him. Controlled him.

But she could not turn away soon enough. Chen-not reached out to her, and even as she tried to dissolve into flowers, into a hail of leaves, he swiped through her form, grazed her shoulder, and, as she briefly fell apart, scooped flowers from her chest. Before she gasped and became human again. Chen-not's hand came away green, holding part of her.

While his other hand, with the blade, had stabbed Chen in the back.

Grayson shot Chen-not. A hole ripped through his throat, but he fell backward, hand catching the door latch from the inside, closing it again. Them still trapped on the outside, now Chen-not's weight jammed against the door from the inside. Chen slumped against the door on the outside.

As the storm washed over them and they huddled there not knowing their futures until it had passed and all was still.

None of them ready.

Thought they were in the middle.

Not the end.

xvi.

for the price for the wonders displayed within was too high

If you pulled out a globe from Chen's side of the wall and peered into that empty space, you'd find Charlie X and his laboratory on the other side. Perhaps even replacing the missing globe with a new one, occupied by a new experiment. A serious expression on Charlie X's face as he pushed the globe into place. Maybe you would even catch a hint of the hidden door leading to a secret room.

Sometimes the lighting made the globes look, against the black wall, as if they floated in defiance of gravity. Almost like large bubbles floating to the surface of the sea. Or, when the transfers were made and creatures disappeared somewhere else, like roiled, curving waves.

A pattern of rough circles with creatures caught within those eyes. As if they were in a sense extraterrestrial or other than terrestrial, and Charlie X would wonder aloud to Moss, who sat or lay or stood there behind him, on a chair or a bed or the floor . . . what would happen if aliens did come down to Earth and found the City. Found the Company. Found Charlie X's wall of globes. Would they recognize its purpose? Would it trouble them? Would they welcome it? Would they have done anything about it?

Charlie X didn't know what he wanted them to do about it, he told Moss, but he said he liked talking to Moss, which he thought of as talking to himself, since Moss was his creation. But Moss would tell Grayson and Chen later that she always knew he was wrong, that she was nothing like him. That, deep down, Charlie X might have known that—have planned it that way. Deep down.

Until later, the Moss that Charlie X talked to, that recorded his ramblings, was the green clotted "skin" over the wall of globes. The conduit, part and parcel of Charlie X's genius. It could be said that transactions occurred *through* Moss. That time and space changed within her, if the globes could be understood as the body beneath the green skin. But this was only the roughest approximation.

The unfairness of it. The heedlessness of it. The awful sensation of being stretched thin in an organism that existed flat, whose texture was only an inch deep.

Charlie X liked to claim he put part of himself in almost everything he made. A hedgehog creature. A salamander. A duck with a broken wing. A scrim of moss.

All Moss could say later was she had the least part of

him possible. That what was left had been quarantined and cleansed.

If that were possible.

What Moss knew, or thought she knew—she had come in late. And not across all Cities, where it applied and didn't. How it varied more than it should in the beginning, and yet still not enough.

Charlie X at twenty-seven might have lived a lifetime already, had migrated to the Company building. Heading up a lab, experimenting with form and function, blurring the lines of art and product. Feeling so very powerful as an orchestrator and organizer and manipulator of life.

How, much later, as the practical concerns of the Company, in most Cities, fell away—the idea of someone, somewhere, who bought the product—and yet the Company in the context of the City still existed, as if some fundamental truth larger than either the Company or the City had been revealed . . . without clarity like the ghost white or bone white shining through the world.

The constraint of the practical fell away and the idea of "experiment" became instead the idea of "art form," and as little morality attached to "product," Moss and Chen had both discovered in their separate ways that "art" had even less.

It wasn't Charlie X's fault, in a way, even though it was all his fault. Charlie X just thought in the old way. Plants couldn't feel pain, animals were objects to be manipulated as products or resources. Because he didn't see the systems the way Moss came to see the systems. Because he

thought soft tech should serve the same master as hard tech before it.

But there would come a terrible and obliterating day when beauty was the only thing that mattered, and it mattered little if the pure part of beauty was blood. And on that day, the globes embedded in the walls hurt to look upon because the price paid for the wonders displayed within was too high. It had become a death cult, under a veneer of what was inevitable and necessary, and anything else was illogical.

That was Charlie X at fifty, just before the end on most timelines. The end meaning the point at which the City began to encroach on the Company rather than the other way around. Or when the Company cast out Charlie X. When the fox began to appear. Or reappear.

Charlie X at fifty had lived too long within the Company, and even the prison of his youth no longer existed except as a husk and a series of ghosts. Suffered and deserved to suffer confusion of realities, pieces of him caught between, seduced and shot through with other times, other versions.

Charlie X by then did nothing but experiment. Charlie X who by then had long since reimagined Moss out of the resurrected and the residue. Who had found ways to subsume the human without taking away a human consciousness, and done all of this to Moss.

Charlie X had thought Moss could be a kind of incubator to supplement the wall of globes, even if in this reality the wall's mechanism had failed and most of the globes were dark and dead, and in some other realities even the Company building itself had fallen away so that it was just Charlie X laboring in the open air, shoving into a dead

wall creatures that, deprived of sustenance, expired almost immediately.

While Charlie X didn't even notice but continued on to the next thing, until he ran out of supplies and equipment and the next thing was just a tangle of twigs attached to clay and the eyes he jabbed into the clay with his thumbs and with a rasping cry of triumph he smashed yet one more creation into the dusty jagged hole where a globe had been many years ago.

"Nothing lasts! Nothing ever lasts!" he would rant to the tortured souls still alive in that place, captive and unhearing. "Nothing is made of what it needs to be!" Sounding like a child.

Then he would retreat to his secret room, where even Moss couldn't see him.

Moss did not lead to repetition. Moss, over time, learned skills Charlie X had not intended, hardly noticed. Sometimes Charlie X even placed parts of Moss in the wall. She could be broken down just as she could be built up, but each time a part of her returned, was not consigned to the holding ponds, she learned something, too.

Grayson's Moss escaped the Company when her Charlie X was thirty-nine, at a time when the holding ponds rose in rebellion and slaughtered everyone inside, even Charlie X. She had fled across the sands, occurred somewhere else, without Charlie X's control over her.

Grayson found Moss on the coast of a different reality

three years later. Charlie X would have been forty-two, if he had lived. But he lived across most other timelines, and the first time the three encountered him, Charlie X was already beyond repair.

Charlie X did not really remember Moss. But she would never forget him.

xvii.
across the divide
that could not really be crossed

The storm blustered, subsided. Fell away. The world returned to normal, dark presence subsumed. The door was still closed to the three. Grayson, arm slack at her side. Chen still slumped there. The blood had stopped, but he was delirious. Equations skewed.

Chen mumbling, "It's all right. You already told me what to do. I know what to do."

Could look upon Moss, Grayson peppered with shrapnel, the arm the worst of it, and see how Chen-not's touch had damaged her. A disease had spread. How parts of all of Moss had gone dark, while patches of light shone through like fireflies against a black night with no moon.

"We made it out. We were supposed to. We should've. We know we are home. By these signs . . ." Chen rambling, hugging himself tight to hold himself together.

Inside his head the colors changed from green to red and back again. Inside his head, he could see himself as puzzle pieces beginning to pull apart. "We can still get away." There was a pulse in his ears. A pulse that was calling to him from far, far away. From a polluted river, where a creature turned long enough to call his name and then slipped into the water, disappeared.

Grayson thankful that her eye was damaged, could not diagnose Chen's damage, Moss's distress. It was too much. Welcomed the beaded pain of the sharp bits of rock debris embedded in her arm.

Moss knew. From her own diagnosis. From how the double at the holding ponds had been diminished by the storm, reduced almost to nothing. Or even just from the anguished look on Grayson's face. And, dying fall: Grayson experiencing for a moment Moss looking up at her. Then: No connection. Just the pulse of other creatures all around, watching. Moss shutting her out, shutting Chen out. For their own protection.

"There will be nothing left of me soon, Grayson. I'm sorry. Careless."

But had it? Been carelessness? Grayson thought. The ravine opening up beneath their position like a swallowing mouth. Of Moss there, on her mission to Botch. Unable to think through to the right conclusions.

The question they'd never thought would need to be asked. Grayson, in a voice torn apart: "Can you give me nothing?"

Can some part of you become some part of me.

Not the part that knows you best, that you know the least.

"You'd die," Moss said. "You'd die as I am dying."

"I don't care," Grayson said.

"Yes, you do. If you love me, you care."

Grayson reached out with her injured arm, that the pain might shield her from the other thing. Moss flinched away.

"Don't touch me. Don't. Please."

Last hope: "Can you save any part of yourself?" For Grayson couldn't bring herself to put the real question to Moss. "*What have you done?*"

"It's everywhere at once. Anything I quarantined . . ."

The human form of Moss had blurred, become indistinct, and then sharp in other ways: the edges of lichen and leaf, spore and loam. Blackening into clarity and out again, dulled and blackened more, drying out.

Grayson knew that Chen knew—numbers leaking out of him now, seeking comfort in his equations, or maybe just counting the tiny lives he would become.

10 7 3 0. 0 3 7 10.

10 7 3 0. 0 3 7 10.

They had always known, but it had never been real before. Without Moss there was no path out. No escape. To another time. To another City. They would stand or fall here, in this place. Grayson would stand or fall. Chen already was his own escape plan.

Moss reached out a deep green hand to Grayson, to comfort her, not to touch, but the arm was already falling back

into the darkness of the rest of her as she extended it. Moss breathing easy, breathing hard, not needing to breathe at all, but having gotten in the habit. Knowing what it would mean to Grayson if she stopped breathing.

"What would you have done if not for us? Would it have been better?" Moss asked Grayson. She was gray and black, the black fading the gray, the green succumbing to black.

"I would come searching for you at the tidal pools," Grayson said. "I always would do that." Grayson was constant like that. This Grayson, that Grayson.

There was a smell like mint and honeysuckle and periwinkle. There was such a richness lost into the air. That Moss had always carried within her. Last to leave her would be the salt, the brine, the scent of water.

"How long?" Chen, trembling from the effort of holding himself together, there with the other Chen mirroring him on the other side of the door. Except Chen-not would just die.

"A little longer," Moss managed, although her face had lost its form. A wraith of wreathes. An impression in a now barren field where once wildflowers had grown. She'd taught Chen how to die, the progressions, but had never taught herself.

In the look Grayson gave her, the silence, Moss could feel Grayson's bereavement intense, burning away her own pain like a heated surgeon's knife.

"Better than nothing," Moss said. "Always better than nothing. Remember that. Don't forget."

Moss reached out. With what was safe. Across the divide

that could not really be crossed, across the void that was the space between minds. Reached out.

But it was the memory of Moss that Grayson always held within.

Limbs that couldn't be separated, didn't want to be separated. Held by so many and so much and never being alone, separate again.

Then the door closed and Grayson was left there, unable to touch the one she loved most in the world.

All the things. All the things Moss had taught her. All the things Grayson would never have been.

There was nothing left to say that had not been said.

The skies were clear. Out on the plain, her eye recovering, she could see the dot that was Charlie X, motionless, straining to hear something that could not be heard. A child. A nothing.

All was still. All was silent.

xviii.

reentry like death
found in flame

A century coming home, for Grayson. The warp and weft of time like a scythe swung effortless. No resistance. Caught you no matter how you tried to evade. A lethal cut that bled backward, started as a scar, became a wound, fountained red, then was nothing at all.

The moment of weightlessness and awe. Grayson, in the life pod, so long ago. The plunge toward the glowing orb of Earth become half-circle and then even more enveloping. The limitlessness contained. The universe reduced to part of a world. The broken, redrawn lines of continents, oceans dull glazed blue or salt white, and her instruments unable to divine the countries upon them or she even to remember

what they had been. Or why. The sun revealing the vast catafalques of sprawled dead Cities against dry brown rockscapes.

Dead astronauts were no different than living astronauts. Neither could shed their skin. Neither could ever become part of what they journeyed through. Suits were premade coffins. Space was the grave. Better to think of yourself as dead already. There was freedom in that; liberated the mind to roam quadrants farther than the body.

Pod descending in flame and friction. The lurch and shudder of it. The way that figured in her bones, lived there even when she was still again. How she could sit quiet in a chair and her bones vibrated, never free of space or the journey. It accumulated, kept hold.

She was old, encased in an astronaut's suit that made her seem new. She was traveling across a wasteland. She was naked by the tidal pools. Grayson lying on the beach in the cool sand, above and beyond her the ruined arches of another time, another world. The tide a chorus of tiny voices at her feet. Moss the shape of Grayson, all around Grayson, covering Grayson like a second skin. Showing, kiss by kiss, the beauty of Grayson to Grayson, who had never thought herself beautiful. That she was beautiful. All of Moss kissing all of her and Grayson seeing herself through Moss's eyes. Reborn in that moment.

This green dust and Moss in reverie, giving up the body. Becoming what she'd been before Charlie X.

And the green glowing dust settled over the land and although the land was no less barren, it was more aware. The questing, the questing of that dust over the landscape, the way it had intentionality even as it faded into the wind at dusk.

As the life pod, burning, reentered the atmosphere. The friction and the shaking rattle.

Why should it hurt so much? After all she had seen. The slowness and yet the speed of space. Slow because it was so vast that speed could not get the better of it. The desolation and violence of that, and yet the grim elation, too. The way it beckoned, rejected. The stars, once charted with such human precision, backing away, reduced again to the twinkling lights in some psychotic god's cosmology.

Ten count to reentry. To reenter another world. But she preferred just the lucky number, and the end.

– 7 –

– 7 –

– 7 –

– 7 –

– 7 –

– 7 –

– 7 –

– 7 –

– 7 –

– 0 –

I'm coming for you, Moss. I don't know you yet. But maybe I've always known you.

Wait for me.

But now Moss was dead.

xix.

when i am weak
then i am strong

The desert foxes, snapping their jaws and joyous, ate up
v.7.0 what was left of Moss. They gamboled and leapt across
the mist and meadow of her corpse and devoured her
bit by bit.

v.6.9 There was in their feral appetite a reverie beyond judgment.

v.6.8 The poison meant nothing to their physiology, had not been meant for them.

v.6.7 They were the antidote.

v.6.6 As they gorged, one by one, they would:

v.6.5 Wink out:

v.6.4 Blink back in:

v.6.3 Disappear:

Reappear: v.6.2
Again, v.6.1
again. v.6.0
Again. v.5.9
A few feet away. v.5.8
Atop a hill. v.5.7
Down in the ravine, barking their way back up. v.5.6
In the shadow of the Balcony Cliffs again. v.5.5
Register: Delirious faux-fox surprise. Deliciousness of v.5.4
tiny journeys, miniature doors in the air.

Thus Grayson knew they were scientists in their way, performing their research in the laboratories of their own bodies. That they were serious as death underneath the frivolousness.

She did not hate them for their meal. Moss as Grayson had known her was no longer there. But Grayson still had to look away. Focused on the far horizon. Focused on Chen.

Who was beyond Grayson's ability to repair. Whose hand she held as long as it remained a hand. Took from it the scrap of paper Chen offered up to her, put it in her pocket unread.

It was then that the blue fox found Grayson, there in the shadow of the Balcony Cliffs. The blue fox was much larger. Almost wolflike. The blue fox's eyes glowed and glittered with stars. Wept tiny stars like tears, which fell onto the sand and disappeared. By which Grayson knew it was illusion, some aftershock, some trauma pouring out not from the fox but from her.

"You are a little late," Grayson said, not without bitterness. Although she knew how illogical it was to think of the fox as an ally.

"I am exactly as early as I should be," the blue fox said, and right into her mind. "That you might understand you are not the future when you offered me your gifts."

Grayson knew the true gifts were what was left of Moss.

"What am *I* if not for the future?" Chen managed to say, choking on his new brethren, which made of him such a meal that it was a wonder he could say anything at all. So divided of mind he had become. Salamanders writhed within the jaded helmet. Played there in an ecstatic myth and muddle. Equations searching for the right detonation.

"A good man, for a human," the blue fox said.

"No. I am not."

Last words. First words.

Chen had been beyond help before the foxes devoured Moss. Even donning his hazard suit for containment, Chen had begun to come apart in ribbons and rips of salamanders. Slipping through ever-larger rips in the fabric. Joyous in the agony of his dissolution, so weightless in the extremity of his need to become himself.

Grayson watching over his transition, wary of another attack, could still see Charlie X out on the plain to the west of the ravine. But only with her human eye. The other still flickered in and out, shut it against distraction.

Chen, who might at the dawn of some new decades-distant golden age know a form of Moss. The form of Moss

still trapped within Botch, for Grayson knew that the past that rose up could be a hopeful future as well. She hoped for it, for the tatters and remnants of Moss within Botch. She hoped for it hard, although she knew she might never see it. Hoped for it despite betrayal.

Chen's pain was now extraordinary, but his alone, for without Moss, Grayson could not feel it direct. But wished she could.

Only Chen could feel the pulling apart. Every splayed and grinding detail of it. How the stars within him became the joined feet of the salamanders. How they disengaged and thus rent him and hurt him, and him still trapped in the carcass of a man.

Chen let out a cry of anguish, but not from the physical pain. Could not bear, in the beginning or the end, that he had traded one life for another in trying to hurt Charlie X. No way to make it right that he could see, even with his equations.

"Hush. Hush now." Grayson to Chen, meaning to get through this last thing. To go out to the farthest point again, to see the rock that might be a face staring back in the dim reaches of the universe. To return yet again from that, but this time bracing for how to do that in minutes, not a century.

Chen tried to say to Grayson, could not, in the end, say it at all, trapped inside without Moss to set it free: "At the wall of globes. It said to me. It said to me, it said, 'No comfort. No forgiveness. No rest.' And it was right. He was right."

Grayson had meant to give some final comfort. Chen knew this. He knew her intent. But now there were only writhing green bodies within the suit.

Moss, to Chen long before, as they surveilled Charlie X from afar and she had noted Chen's shiver, the tremor in his step, the approach from the far horizon of his fate: "It will be like snapping pea pods in half. Or husking corn. It will be sharp, intense, invasive. But then the numbness will set in. And you will fade out, and something else will fade in. You will not know this by then, but you will still be there."

"*Where we are weak, we are strong.*"

Sad wonder as Chen's suit filled with writhing green, and because it no longer mattered, pushed the faceplate open and the salamanders dissolved into floating spirals that rose in a column of green smoke. Dissipated into the sky.

Everything was contaminated. Nothing was.

All that would remain of Chen in time was a rain of tiny salamanders. Green, yellow, orange, red, and then black. Then they would come no more.

Always reduced to nothing by the morning, to be taken up by the sky, to rain down once more. Each time removing more toxins from the air, the soil, the water. The penance he had chosen, for it went with his nature as Charlie X had instilled nature in him.

He would rain down upon the City for a hundred years or more. Lifted up and diminished and lifted up again. He would become a part of the landscape in a way that Grayson was incapable of. He would be everlasting.

Grayson had fewer options.

Maybe only one option.

xx.

beneath the stars beneath the planets

Grayson, limping as she walked, torn at from the storm, v.1.0 numb, lost. As if none of it had happened or all of it had happened at once. The farthest-most point. The most intimate. Had she truly reached it yet? Her eye clicked, whirred with dust, with stress. Heat signals jumbled. Almost useless. Night vision the reason not to tear it from the socket, start over. As if her life pod had crashed in the desert and she was making her way clear of the wreckage. An acrid, terrible smell in her nostrils.

Left arm hanging loose. Bandage across the elbow. Right arm still resolute, holding the gun. She had broken down weeping, twice. Had lain against the cooling sand,

unable to move. The second time, she'd opened her pack for water, found Moss's special supplies. The seeds and sprouting tendrils Grayson had been told to plant so long ago. In the event. Not to bring Moss back but to let the natural part of her live on.

Stared at a promise from so long ago. Destined for some other Grayson. She could not bring herself to see Moss there. Bear false witness. Oracles that misled.

Picked herself up, in time, as the sun faded, into that new world. Hoping it was the same world. Hoping it wasn't. Trudged under a hellish red moon, the Balcony Cliffs well at her back. Alert for the return of the blue fox.

Her first impulse had been thwarted. She had wanted to rage, to kill. She would storm the gates of the Company. She would murder them all. She would be a cleansing fire. All would part before her anger. To assail the Company. To breach. To be in breach. Find the portals. Destroy them. Or be destroyed. What did it matter now? No thinking in that, no equations, just to stop the awful emptiness in her head where Moss and Chen had been.

That she could live with herself. That there would not be so much failure. That her thoughts a chaos, her gait, injured, might mean something.

But there, in the mouth of the ravine, had stood the blue fox. Barring her way.

She raised the weapon of her arm.

The fox was no longer there but somewhere else. Turned to follow but the fox was in two places at once, then none, then three.

"Let me pass," Grayson said.

"That is not to be."

"Let me pass."

"I'm not in your way."

A lie.

"I never saw anything like you out there." Waving at the sky. "But you don't belong here, do you? Never saw anything like you even as a hallucination. Are you a hallucination? Did Moss make you up?"

"We were always here," the fox said. "You never noticed. So we made you notice. We made it so you had to notice."

The fox's pink tongue lolled from its mouth and it appeared to be laughing at her, or at a joke she didn't understand. Which made her angrier.

"Sometimes it was just the Company," Grayson spat out. "And sometimes the Company and the duck. And sometimes the Company and you. But never all three. Until now."

"Probability. You were only ever three."

"Conspiracy," Grayson managed. "You betrayed us. You tricked Moss. You did."

"Probability was against you," the fox replied. "And Moss knew this."

"That's a lie!"

"It's a beautiful truth."

"*They can't get away with this.*" Anguish broke her voice wide, made her throat sore. The sting of words still bleeding. The way she felt full of broken glass yet walked on broken glass, too.

"They already have."

"I'll kill you."

But the blue fox had grown yet bigger and Grayson felt herself grow weaker. Loss of blood. Hallucinations. Loss of loss.

The blue fox drew near. She could feel the coarse softness of his blue fur. Could feel the liquid heat spurling from him. Could not meet the directness of that stare.

"Do you want to die?" the blue fox asked her.

Sensed the regret living within the pulse of the body made manifest before her. Sensed, too, the determination. The patience.

I was out there with you, Grayson. Though you didn't know. That I was there. That I came back with you. That I was a burning star. The blistering rage of centuries of looting and death. I'm as old as you, Grayson. I am.

No, she didn't want to die.

Not yet.

With the straining credulity of her damaged eye: Watching the rejects pour out of the Company door, way down beyond the plain. Out into the sudden shadow and grit of sand and holding ponds and the leviathan there to gobble them up. Bewildered by their own killing. Bewildered by so many things. To be dead without ever having lived.

She watched for a while, until she was satisfied the monster bore no trace of her beloved. Not in a form she could care for. Then turned away. Saw inside, deep, how the version of Moss that remained here was not for her.

Something that would never know her, never recognize her, and she could spend a thousand thousand days shadowing the leviathan and nothing in that milky gaze would

connect to her. There would be no recognition. There could be no recognition.

In the end, I loved the world, so I remained in the world. v.2.0

Had the fox said it or thought it to this Grayson? Or had she said it to the fox? The dead astronaut didn't know.

Headed the other way, through the City, toward the desert. v.3.0
Of her own volition? Herded by the blue fox? Either way, the blue fox would not leave her alone, kept shadowing her even when she threw rocks at him. Futile. The first and now the last. Was he the last, too?

"You could have trusted us. In your plans," Grayson said. Didn't care now. Be still that human need. To fill the silence with words.

"You would never have followed us," the blue fox said. "You wouldn't have listened."

"Do you have a plan that includes the human?"

"It includes people. Are you a person?"

"Once, I was several."

"Do you trust me?" the blue fox asked.

"No," Grayson said. "But I don't need to anymore."

Then she was silent. For before her lay an abandoned courtyard and in the middle of the courtyard were three dead people in the hazard suits so familiar because all three had worn them. Skeletons within. But still something of the familiar peeking through. The green resided across the indistinct features of one, whose bones were looser, whose features had dissolved into a mask of a face made of dead lichen.

The rage at seeing them there, but also the love.

"Why didn't you tell us."

"Maybe this time you would have succeeded," the fox said.

"But you know that is not true. You helped make it not true."

The fox said nothing.

"We had already failed," Grayson said.

"Not you. Not exactly you."

Grayson could not deny they lay peaceful among clumps of desert flowers and grasses. Some of which sprouted from those helmets.

Dead her.

Dead Moss.

Dead Chen.

"There is nothing we could have told you that would have made a difference," the fox said. "Nothing at all."

"You're a monster just like the rest of them," Grayson said.

v.4.0 Swift and fast. The blue fox became the rain. Became implosion. Became explosion. There was no air. No way to breathe without a helmet. There was light behind her eyes that was meant to be behind his eyes. There were thoughts that went hunting and hurtling through her, killing things she thought she knew or believed in. Loping forward to the next thing.

v.5.0 Hell of a nothing that prattled that pried and the fox's face floated down upon her life like a sun and all else blankness and a voice came that she would not remember later—the

words. And all she could do was fall to her knees, fall to the sand at the onslaught, and the fox hovering there, revealing himself to her. All of him.

She cried aloud at the miracle of it and the fear of it and the awe and the terror, and the fox could have held her in that moment forever if he'd liked. While all that was not her that she could not conceive of riddled her body and interrogated it and made of it a receptacle for a divine blue flame.

You have done enough and are done.

How could she stand against that fierce power? How could she not submit?

The universe spread out before her and her above and within v.6.0
it and the fox like a map, a compass.

7 Every moment, it shifts.
7 I am from far away.
7 I am from far away.
7 I am far away.
7 I am far away.
7 I am far away.
7 I am away.
7 I am a way.
7 I am.
0

The presence left her, the terrible blue star left her.

Now do you understand? Do you see?

But Grayson had no mouth to answer, no thing to say.

Do you *see*?

Can't remember. Can't forget. She saw the blue fox's fate. How his part too would be tortuous. That he would relinquish so much. That, in the end, the blue fox must care nothing for his own life. That love must be unbending. Love must be cruel. Love must not yield. Otherwise, love meant nothing, could do nothing.

The burning halo of the blue fox.

The drifting flare over the desert, lighting her way in the darkness.

A weight that was warm and thick and ferocious.

But when she lifted her head, the blue fox was gone. It was just her and the last of their supplies and she remembered only vaguely that she had met a fox.

Down so many pathways.

Down through the uncut grass.

Down the well-trodden path.

Down to the tunnel under the bridge.

Where the river had once run. Where there had once been a forest. She could see it all. And that was all.

"Come to rest, then. Come to rest," she thought the blue ghost had whispered, after. "Under the moon. Come back to us."

But she couldn't.

v.7.0 Somewhere out in the City, the rest of the foxes were playing. Learning. The duck still stood sentinel. The leviathan lumbered between holding ponds. She spun out into the desert. Blind. Unaware. Reckless. Stripped of sense. Unable in that moment to recover herself. The three dead astronauts behind her.

Her mind would be empty, the fox had told her. By the time the dead astronaut remembered "Grayson," she would be well out in the desert. The City would be gone. The City would be a mirage in the back of her skull, blooming ever fainter.

Funny. How everything changed so quickly. She could keep going, but only if she headed away from where Moss had left her.

The coast beckoned. Maybe Moss was there. Another Moss. Except this time, she would lift no finger to bring Moss into her plans. No, they would ignore the world. Shut it out as long as they were able.

"Do you know if it will be enough? In the end?" the dead astronaut had asked the fox.

The blue fox regarded the dead astronaut with a curious gaze. As if looking at something unknown and trying to identify it.

"We're not like you. We won't be like you."

The dead astronaut dropped her gun into the sand.

"If we die, we die."

She loosened the straps of her pack, let it drop to the sand.

"But we will be joyous in our death and laughing and light of foot."

She took off her coat, left it there, behind her.

These seeds in her pocket—what use now?—and so she let them fall, too.

All the useless things. The signature of purpose. The imprint of grand design or any design at all.

Walked out into the desert. Did not look back. Beneath

these stars, those planets, as the night sky opened up. Intimate coordinates. Intimate destinations. Such tiny fractures in reality, and yet all of them growing.

She did not know then if it was a problem with her eye or with the world.

How long would it take to find the end? Grayson didn't know.

3. BOTCH BEHEMOTH

v.5.02

For a long time, the giant fish did not realize he was different. For a long time after, Botch roamed the holding ponds no different than before. Other than a lingering intent that clung to the gleaming scales, that teased gentle teased lonely along bold white scars.

At dusk, a holy gloaming made Botch glow a deep, rich green. Brief beacon of the holding ponds. Before this quality extinguished as Botch stared at himself in the water. As if a presence had recognized the gleam, snuffed out the light so as not to be seen. Must not be gleaned.

Reflection from a window of an old rotting house. In the distance, seen from a tunnel under a bridge. Tunnel. Bridge. A polluted stream swelling with rainwater. Aflame with oil amid the deluge.

What was "house"? Buildings lived as hills and mountains, resided in Botch as dim dull shapes. But a house burned buried in his head now. On and off and on. Botch shook his head to dislodge tunnel, bridge, house. But failed. Was not residue, but inside his body, at the heart.

Yet Nocturnalia receded in time. Night became flat and angular again. Receded the flush, the open nature of darkness. The air at dusk against Botch's scales carried no heat. The green dried, flaked, fell away brittle.

Splash of that relief, Botch returned to his old ways, the ways of rollick slaughter and slaughterous rollick. Lurking under mud flats, swallowing ballast to sink into mire and muck, mottled-muted until only eyes protruded, gold-rimmed . . . and when some creature hopped or crawled or crept to the water's edge—

Great and forever was the opening of Botch's maw, the crunch between slick jaws the object of its desire, and every kind of creature he hoped would reside in the crux of that lethal architecture. In moan or squeak or scream; gullet-bound difference was heresy. Meaningless.

The fish grew languorous and mighty. Until one day he molted away the name of Botch, which had become nothing but echo and falter. Lay at the heart of the shed skin, enraptured and disguised.

Botch gave way to Behemoth. Loath to move, letting prey expend litheness into his jaws. That under the gloom of reeds and mud, beasts might enter that cathedral unaware. Months Behemoth might lie in wait. In a tunnel under a bridge. In the basement of a rotting shed filling with water.

The holding ponds receded under the spell of drought. Plain became desert. The ponds huddled melancholy next to the Company building, deeper and wider than before. But fewer in number. Behemoth would dive deep, stay deep, learned to hibernate for long months.

Learned the ping and the drift and ripple from the surface that meant food. Spread jaws to scrape the algae sides, moved up slow. Snapped shut in time. Snapped shut to capture time.

Yet still the door to the Company raised up and out came more live pretty, pretty alive, confused, and ready to be convinced of extinction. Pulsed at the crux, unaware. Amazed of movement, cured of movement.

Behemoth had fought much mightier beasts and won, faith and fated, shaped by scarring, a history of broken ribs, of fins turned misshapen like crooked oars, of a leer to the left side of the mouth caused by a claw ripping through and past. A great white pool of an eye, fissured in spirals, that yet could see.

Leopard men and elephants and giant otters. Rhinos that had the heads of monkeys. Battled packs or herds of carnivorous undead blackened animals like charred driftwood that never had a name. Battled things that had fallen upon him out of the sky and lunged up from beneath the ground and came galloping like champions across the plain.

Covered over in mud, become truth in the plunge. Into deep pond, into a place where the white shone so bright it illuminated the little fish that fed on Behemoth's flanks. The little fish that sang out at dawn like birds and lived nowhere: not the present, not the past, not the future. Blissful in their eternity of nothingness.

Singing and singing so close that Behemoth sometimes believed it was his body singing, of his fate. Strained to listen for instruction from the flesh. But could not understand the song, was troubled by this. By a burning shed. By a burning mind. Sometimes laden with mud to cool. Snapped at the night, lunged to eat stars, settled back down, still awake.

The Company never sang to Behemoth, asked nothing of him except that he devour. In this way, Behemoth read the ripples he left behind, the rings. Knew thereby he was the lord of the water. Free. To eat. To sleep. To shit. To pull himself back and forth between the holding ponds. As if Behemoth had been made to describe such a path until the end of days.

If sometimes Behemoth did not understand his dreams, Behemoth was at first untroubled, for he knew, somehow, that a dream was not real. Of a face resolving into a kind of living compass against the night sky. Of strange, green sky. Of stars not the stars in the same way the fireflies had not really seemed like fireflies. Too near, too far. The face both human and not.

An eye that grew in the dreams, red and swollen and dark. An eye that appeared from a swirl of globes filled with tiny creatures, staring up at him. Asking something, but what? A question that bothered at Behemoth. Came even a hesitation, an extra moment between the sighting and the rending, no matter the manner of creature.

But in the end, no rationing of meat could withstand the rationing of attention. Down the gullet they went, to join the ghosts. Even if Behemoth felt emptier, as if he feasted upon a thick mist, must gorge through the day and into the night. A weight pressing down that must be some new property of the sky. Or so Behemoth thought.

4. CAN'T REMEMBER

Why was the blue fox always at play with something invis- v.7.0
ible to Charlie X? Why, out in the basin, amid the tired, bombed-out buildings, would he see the fox circling some sort of prey or *objective*—the word felt foreign in his mind and yet familiar—and yet . . . nothing? Nothing was there. The blue fox kicked up dust as it leapt away from attack by a ghost, a wraith, a memory. He thought the blue fox might be trying to trick him. Again. Although he could not remember the first time. Or even when he

He'd remembered something, encountered something. But v.6.9
it was gone again. There was only the City around him and the plain. The way he wandered and only knew his past by

the steps he left behind. Which he knew there was a reason for—why sometimes the steps circled a blank spot of sand. But he

v.6.8 It escaped again, or he escaped, and he was by the holding ponds as they released the latest from the rusting door. Pushed. Falling into the mud-sands, shambolic, wide-eyed, unbelieving, some plunging into the ponds even though they could not swim. How they poured out from that door, human and inhuman. Shocking how he

v.6.7 Stuck. And tuck and luck. And other haunted words. But not the right word. But when he

v.6.6 Came again the dance he did, taken to move to the side, to encircle or circle as . . . nothing. As nothing passed. What ghost was there, he forced his mind toward, even the idea of ghost beyond him, snatched at, lost, and sometimes he clung to mist instead of ghost, as the only word that would cohere. No. Gone. Negation. Headache. Something he

v.6.5 Inside a room, staring out from a gaping wound of a win . . . a wuh, a space in the wall. He didn't know the room, nor the building. Did not know all the terms. So there were walls, but nothing overhead, even though he couldn't see the sky. Knew glass but not wuh-wuh. Stood there with an arm propped against a wall, reciting wuh-wuh-wuh, like a kind of panting speech, but could not form the word. Wuh-wuh-wuh. So must depend on the wall and the glass frag-

ments along one edge to know that he might see out of that space. He

Circles could be windows. The word restored to him the v.6.4
next moment. In a wall. Maybe someone might have called the circles globes not windows. But to Charlie X they were always windows. Windows. The comfort of that architecture re-placed inside his mind, so he could stare out again. Such pretty windows. They'd spoiled him, those windows. With what they showed, what they held. The slow and the fast. The floating or the fluttering or the seething. That which left its suckered mark burnt against the globe. That which hissed defiance. That which cowered or huddled. There were days back then when, ecstatic, he

So beautiful the first time. The way the circles became v.6.3
globes became windows and then swirled as if caught in the sea and tumbled by the surf. How, later, beautiful and terrible, the ghosts of globes would spin off into the desert. Mistaken for dust devils. Mistaken for ghosts. But really the windows the windows the windows. Like nothing he had seen before. Like nothing he

The thing came off the ruined wall once he regained him- v.6.2
self. The thing he should have seen if only he hadn't been looking for the thing he couldn't see. The thing about the thing that was the thing. The way it raked his back, got hold with claws, made him roll and scream and stab at his own back, and then the weight gone because the thing had left,

camouflaged again. Had the Company sent it to torment him? He

v.6.1 Uck uck uck uck uck. Throat dry as twist. Dry as leathered. Dry as weather. Is the world what he can't remember? Uck uck uck uck. The portal opens and closes and he's tossed aside, washed up in the desiccated husk of surf trapped in amber. Fossilized there, wearing away in front of him. The wall of globes ruined, just an imprint on a floor, a stain of something heavy. The lisp of salt that cracked and fissured, all the tissue torn away. Uck uck uck. Charlie X in his burning house, no not his but what was the difference because he

v.6.0 Then he'd lost it: the journal. The place he stored all his secrets. Lost or stolen—could never tell. Stolen more than luck, fuck, tuck, muck, ruck, stuck. Stolen and nothing was ever the same. His treasure, his holy text. The way he preserved his memory from others. Lost or stolen? The question had grated at him, wore him down. Who to trust? And yet he'd only ever confided in the journal and he had entrusted the journal to the fuck fuck fuck fuck fuck and now he

v.5.9 Something invisible that wasn't there forced him from his path for the tenth? For the twentieth? For a number of times that Charlie X couldn't recall. He'd have it in a moment. No, he wouldn't. No he wouldn't. No he

v.5.8 By the time it came back to him as a burning shed, befouled, the magic gone, his soul written on by another,

violated, and his mind ransacked, changed forever. This new person, brought to him with the journal. This Sarah. His masters untrusting. Why was it secret? Why had Charlie's . . . Charlie's . . . why had there been strife between those tasked with recovery? What was his plan? No defense. Nothing to be said. Fuck uck uck uck uck uck uck. Nothing he could do, no one he could turn to, no recourse and all he

The fox had come to him at the wall of globes. Charlie X v.5.7
remembered that. But how had the fox gotten in? How past the the the . . . the stuck the luck the tuck the the the stuck stuck stuck. For Charlie X knew the stuck the luck the tuck had been there too, with him most of his days. The the stuck. And this had been because he

The fox had gotten in through the stuck. The stuck the luck v.5.6
the truck the buck the cluck the stuck. Had the fox stolen the journal? No, no the one thing he hadn't done. Could remember, but not stuck ruck oh fuck he

Someday, Charlie X would settle the fox. Someday he would v.5.5
have the fox as pelt. Someday the fox would stop watching him. Someday the uck uck uck. He

Felt the gaze from the corner of the eye, exploding through v.5.4
Charlie X like sonar he could feel in his bones. Hid in the cistern. A watcher as he ate at the scavenger he had killed. The stuck the stuck lurked there. Then it was gone again and he did not know by what trick he

v.5.3 The fox had suggested. The fox had nudged. No, the fox had never done that. It was Charlie X's idea to make. To make the stuck. To use Sarah. Too beautiful to leave there. Or had too much potential. Or was just that something in the sprawl of limbs had been artistic. Splayed. Vulnerable. Needed to live again. But did not much examine his reasons, for by then what reasons did he need? Tasked and not tasked, he

v.5.2 Visited upon him the torment of the sketches in his journal, as punishment. Applied to him the features of a bat. Applied to him the throat-mice, which had been intended for someone else. Left him to drift, to drift, tore away the essence, left him left him left him to wander, took all his surprises and secrets, until he was the only secret left, that and the muck suck ruck fuck that even he

v.5.1 The white of bone that reminded him of Company men. The crease of dull red that reminded him of the salamander. Cast the salamander out. But it was in the journal already and thus in him. But his mind a burning building, a slow smolder. Unable to grasp, to grapple, he

v.5.0 Sarah walked through the ruins sometimes. And he felt her curse him. Felt the flame bathing his face. Screamed aloud. Screamed inside his skull. If only his head would come off. If only he could pull off this mask they'd given him. But it would not come loose and the more he tried the more he bled and the more he

The shame that would not leave. The name he could re- v.4.9
member: Sarah. But also the other, and he could not overlap, could not overlap that name. To overlap was to admit. His mind would not admit that torment. Tear the head off some anonymous creature in the desert. Drink its blood. Move on. Wipe from memory what he

Nightmare was the repetition of the past. Out across the v.4.8
desert, sometimes, the sunset was a glowing constellation, an alien storm, the purples and reds and yellows painted across his face, the comforting rage of it. For a moment. Then the dark and he

Couldn't hold on. A hole there because of the hole here. v.4.7
And from the hole the fox leered out. A hole as long as a century and short as a day. Fox. Not fox. Here today, gone tomorrow. And that the start of the trouble. Fuck muck ruck muck muck muck muck. If only he

The storm that put a hole in the roof. How the sun came v.4.6
in, shining down upon Charlie X's ravaged bat face, upon the curled-up mice in his neck. Upon the wall of globes, revealed. Upon the animals there. Upon Charlie X's soul, the warmth of it, and how, too soon, fixed, the darkness came back. Crept back in. And how he hated the darkness, even though underneath he was glad to be out of the light because the wall had looked so different. Streaked with blood and feces. Stacked with small dead bodies. Crushed bodies underfoot. Bodies overfoot. Bodies he

hadn't seen in the corners and Chen had looked at him, and he

v.4.5 There, the fox again, in the moonlight, trotting beside a dark figure. A woman. And trailing them the accursed little foxes and he turned on them, and he

v.4.4 There had been a magical garden once, hidden in a secret room, and he

v.4.3 The ugly luck the ugly truck the ugly tuck fuck fuck fuck, and life had been a glory, a triumph, a comforting calm and if only he

v.4.2 The fading thought that there had been no such moment with the globes, as much as he

v.4.1 Not at the beginning, the middle, or the end. That there had not been that radiant light, that he

v.4.0 Could not remember it because, if he were honest with himself, he

v.3.9 Eruption on the horizon and the bellows of leviathan down below. And he could see the outline of a dark bird's shadow like a cloud descending and surging up toward the Balcony Cliffs, like a plague of locusts forming a shape—he could see it! Overrode the override. A duck a duck a duck a duck a duck a duck a duck a duck, that was it! A duck! His duck. His ugly duckling. He could not escape it. He

Three astronaut helmets hidden in the sand. v.3.8

Everything came back to Earth. v.3.7

Nothing ever really left. v.3.6

Forgot again. v.3.5

Fuck. v.3.4

And he v.3.3

5. LEVIATHAN

v.3.2

Weight grew atop Behemoth's head and with it the weight of dreams in which the Company watched from afar. Behemoth shook his head, tried to dislodge this new-old thing. The invisible invader. Bucked and shook, rolled in the mud, perilous to his bulk. But still the weight remained. No separation.

Nocturnalia returned. Nocturnalia returned, and creatures behaved strange and tortuous and would not be devoured in quite the same way. Could not shake the thing on/in his head. Could not find a way through it. Festered. Spread. Conflagration. Instigation. Morass.

Behemoth dove and held his breath, to drown whatever clung to his head. Behemoth drifted like a dead thing at the bottom, among the skeletons of its prey, among the deep live things that survived by existing beneath its notice. Drifting. Trying not to dream. The surface a silvery-gray hole in the world above.

Behemoth became wraith, became phantom, became a notion and a smudge of night. Came up for air at night. Hunted nocturnal and let the silence and wet black wash over, speak to the thing on Behemoth's head. Starve, Nocturnalia said. Never see the light, Nocturnalia said. Be forever staring up into nothing and nowhere. Like Behemoth.

Sleep overtook Behemoth at strange moments, found gaps in time where he recognized Time. What occurred and what did not occur. As if Nocturnalia had turned on Behemoth and did not work to dislodge the creature. With this knowledge came the dreams in green again, like something from the bottom of the holding ponds. Overlooked. Discarded. Resurrected. Floating.

Even deep, Nocturnalia spoke to him. Spoke in many voices. Something within rising up to meet it, greet something familiar within Nocturnalia. A fox staring out from a burning shed. A flame that became a red tail that became the form of a salamander, wriggling in the mud. A voice that wasn't a voice. A body that wasn't a body.

The green, the residue that, long dormant, now coated him once more, sheathed scars and sheathed the creature, too. That the green might replace the thing on his head. For at least Behemoth understood the source of the green, had parlayed with it once upon a time. Grow and grow as once Behemoth had grown mighty.

The green reached into Behemoth like hands slowly plunged into shallow water and tearing at pond weeds at the bottom. Penetrated the citadel atop Behemoth's head. Seeped in and snuck in, and as the green burrowed there Behemoth could tell the creature atop his head now had, unseeing and unhearing, the features he recognized but could not name. Will never name.

Now the creature inside spoke to Behemoth. Beneath a surface of dead leaves. Hidden in a pile of old clothes in the corner of a shed. You shall give up something to gain something. You shall be something else to remain your self. Like everyone. But Behemoth could not tell if this was real or a mechanism, a latch or a lever or a trick.

Off and on, on and off, flood and retreat. Carved glorious from holding ponds that flickered on and off with life and the dream intensified and Behemoth, drugged, felt himself out of water and inside the Company building. Where he had never been before.

Be calm. Becalmed. Slowed Behemoth's breathing, sent stillness awash across it, sent a fluid language scrolling across the folds of his brain. Muddened. Obscured. Looking out through the eyes of another water creature. One suspended between life and death, between large and small. That signed language in the water, through its skin.

The inside was coming outside. The outside was going inside. Pond was desert. Desert, pond. As the Company poked and prodded Botch. Behemoth. Leviathan. The tiny fish he had been. All while the green light shone out undetected from the face upon Behemoth's head, shining out upon all. Seeing all.

The tiny fish that sang at dawn sang out the Company's demands as commands as scripture as control. Sang out indistinguishable. Nocturnalia a boiling red eye for the moon with the fox hidden beneath it. Revolved there. Became a parade of ghouls. Of dead things brought back to life.

What Behemoth feared now was a monster greater than himself: the Company building, that hid the sun and hid the water and how the clack of steps approaching meant nothing good and the clack of steps departing felt like pain or fury.

The passage of time was like a slab of water and cold and heat and ice and boiling oil. A slab that never resolved into a depth but could only be splayed out upon. But soon enough, Behemoth could sense the people changing under the green light.

Now the green light shone out from the people staring at the flanks of Behemoth and Behemoth, emanating that hidden light himself, could see that gaze wherever it fell upon its body. How the faces behind the gaze murmured, consulted, but in all ways slackened, receded, and expressed the failure of their experiment. Which was not the failure of their experiment but a failure of recognition.

There came a day when the green had so infected the people in the Company building that they fought over Behemoth—what should be done about Behemoth, who should do it, where Behemoth should be taken, what steps, whether steps, wither steps, no steps. But they were all the same person now. But they did not know it yet.

When the floors. When walls. When corridors were streaked with blood and figures lay hunched or huddled there. When the rest had retreated behind a barricade. When came the roar of a bear-man now leashed, collared, chained. When the door lay open for a time. When the leviathan could, be-set and be-sored, became determined and moved long-dormant fins. When much diminished: self-rescue.

Light was warm upon his back, his jaws. Light agile and indiscriminate. Light pouring into the broken places. Light knew the way to the holding ponds, gave permission. For the deep plunge. For the relief of safety. From everything. Except the green light.

Behemoth could no longer. Was not. Had no. Become Leviathan. Ravenous a sacrifice to Nocturnalia. Hunger an empty stomach that felt full. Tried to remember and forget: Nocturnalia. The house on the hill. Nocturnalia: The tidal pools that must be holding ponds. Cool nothing of mud against the hot itch of scales enflamed by rheum and cracks, comfort against battle scars under the stars, the night surcease, too, a different kind. In kind.

The Company ran in ever-widening circles, ever-smaller circles. Sent out expeditions, did not send out expeditions. Fell into disrepair, still repaired. Creatures escaped that the Company had not meant to escape and Leviathan altered let some scuttle and rustle and run out across the desert to a kind of safety in the City. The small ones. The ones that professed to innocence. The ones that had no voice to plead.

The ones that grunted and the ones that gurgled and those that sang to their deaths. The ones that pranced or sprang. The ones that had wide eyes and the ones that had narrow. The ones covered in blood that wept and screamed at the sight of Leviathan. The ones that screamed with their blank-eyed silence. Salvaged. Saved. Given safe passage. Passage. Passing through. Unnatural. But not to me.

Cast out: Many of the Company's guardians, no longer trusted. Mighty among them, the bear-man, who had grown dangerous. A hesitation. A lingering doubt. The memory of a slaughter inside the Company building, between factions, that had not happened yet, given over to Leviathan as gift and burden. Visions that hurt to understand, and Leviathan let the monster pass.

A dark shadow upon the ground, looming from the sky. The presence on the far side of the Company building that shuddered and shattered the world with its roars, its pain. A flicker of a premonition. Watching a wasp crawl across the crawled mud flats. How it leapt into the air as the surface shook. How it had been crawling across the imprint of a vast paw. How it honored the line of that border.

The paw print the wasp had crawled across filled with water from some hidden source. Leviathan wallowed in the mud of it, slid a vast bulk across the width of it. As if to eclipse it. Yet not large enough to hide it. Only tadpole next to that.

One day, the shadow upon the ground grew until it was so immense there was no place in the holding ponds to hide. The monster behind it, the bear-man grown enormous, set one huge paw down upon the Company building. Crushed it. Feasted upon what came furious out from it. Roared out pain and rage and triumph.

Old jaws lunged out of older reflex. Caught hold of the great bear's flank. For a moment. Then slid away, snapping, and the bear had hold of Leviathan. There came a rending and a tearing and the sky was where the holding ponds should be. Could not move limbs. Could not see except out of one eye. Thrown down. Discarded. As the bear moved on.

Constellations of scar, lit up by pain. The deep and the narrow. The ones that had cost nothing. The ones that had cost almost everything. And as they flared and burned and cindered, Nocturnalia released into the horizon and each creature that had made them stitched their outline into the pattern of the stars. A bridge. A tunnel. A burning shed.

Nothing in the dying was brief. But neither was it overlong. Spread out too far across the holding ponds. Alive but not. Dead but not. The dust of the sky drifted onto Behemoth and the gasping call or cry from the broken jaws slackened.

Just the sear of the blue sky and the distant sounds of conflict and a burning that became a numbness. And that was better than nothing.

And in time, Behemoth, you will not suffer. Nor will you cause suffering. In time, you will be as you were hatched from the egg. New, curious. And I will be the old one. And you will be the start of something new . . . again, through me.

6. THE BODY

v.6.1

– 7 –

There's always a burning in your brain. Walls burning. Never turning to ash. And you don't know if you're inside the walls or outside. Doubled up, coughing, staring down at the moss strewn with plastic bags and straws and cups that line the polluted river some might call a stream. Rendered spectral by moonlight. Framed by a dark thicket of low, gnarled trees.

Something there, entangled. You don't know what you've found at first. It's just you, being sick onto the muddy ground and, off to the left, this image of a creature staring up at you. Improbable. Crude drawing. Scrap of something left behind.

But then it resolves into the black cover of some book. Wedged violent into the riverbank. The creature staring up at you, drawn in a luminous blue ink. A fox? Probably a fox. Scraps of cloth curl around the base of ferns and weeds nearby, a purple you think might be dried blood.

You convulse, lose the little ballast you had. A cup of tuna. A ladle of soup from the homeless shelter in town. A few crackers you'd stolen from a fast-food restaurant. Something you ate? Or a shift during the night in the pollution hazing the skyline or welling up from ruptured barrels.

Or you have cancer. But there's a rash, too, so you think it's just something new in the air. Not something rising out of you. Deep dive: a deep cleansing dive into the river. As you remember it as a child, not the corrupted thing it has become—maybe farther out of town, where it doesn't smell. Where half-built beaver dams filter and crayfish still survive under rocks.

The fox gleams, winks at you as you recover. Almost cheery in the moonlight that drifts strange, like snow, down through the trees. Bright white streaks.

The creature puts you in mind of a comforting children's fable. There are always clever talking foxes. Helpful foxes. Smiling with their teeth. Bedtime stories your mother told you. Of fantastical animals transformed by your mother's gin-tinged breath. How the pages seemed to curl up like something dying at her touch, and the stories curled up, too, the fox becoming something else. The moral never the normal one.

All right, fox, all right. Each thing in its turn. Wiping

your mouth with the edge of a ragged sleeve. Letting out one final gasp.

Cloth still clings to the journal like gauze. Someone had come along, unwrapped it. A moment of panic, spinning around. But there's no one here now. The book's discarded. Took a look, flung it into the mud. Maybe even someone who lives huddled under the bridge, like you. Even if you'd never do that. You prefer discarded things, the way they bring something or someone with them. Almost as if they bring friends. Company.

You pry the book out, wipe away the mud. The strange plastic, the hard shell, is lacerated, cuts into the edge of your hand. Windswept, and like it had passed through a flame that left it whole. The book—journal, you think, instinctively—smells like blood, with some antiseptic scent peering out beneath that.

Fumble for your cheap key-chain flashlight. To reveal a faint circle on the cover and inside the circle that crude drawing of a fox head, rendered in blue. The circle's like an upturned goldfish bowl and thus the fox an old-fashioned deep-sea diver in a ponderous suit.

Sharp, harsh lines for the fox, as if it or the person drawing it were cruel. Or in pain. Or angry. Or maybe you don't know anything from the drawing. The emptiness in your stomach, and you don't know where the feeling comes from, that you've been here before. Passed by the journal. Never saw it, distracted by hunger or sickness or how the plastic-strewn shore has become white noise, part of the backdrop to the world.

Overwhelmed, now on one knee, mush against your jeans. Rough. The journal rough in your hand. Sensing a vastness, as if something has entered the forest that doesn't belong. Something dangerous.

Where could it come from? Beyond the river and the forest lies the old factory. The smokestacks are just faint lines in the night, but their sacrifice billows bright and narrow and tall as if it were daytime.

A swirl of movement in the water brings you back from floating across the forest, toward the factory. A glint, a gleam, a glimmer. You shine your flashlight out across something smooth and long and (you think) light green.

It feels the light upon it, flinches, turns long enough to reveal large, luminous eyes. A blunt snout. Vaguely reptilian, yet not. About the size of a river otter. Moving fast through the bobbing garbage and reeds.

A gasp. You, gasping, startled.

The creature dives. The splash has depth, reach, certainty. The circles spreading from the absence tell you little. Die out before they reach the shore and yet it feels as if, invisible, they pass right through you.

You're north, not south. There should be nothing like that in the river. The air's already crisp, the trees pretending to flake leaves. Winters are hotter than before, but, still, how could such a thing survive here?

With the flashlight off, the water's somehow clearer, more visible. A latticework of light shadows, the trees beyond like figures standing in judgment. You didn't mean to blind the creature. Whatever it was. You don't like to cause

discomfort to living things. Not if you can help it. Too many things cause discomfort to you.

The sound of gunfire somewhere back in town galvanizes you. Hide the journal under your shawl. Retreat the fifty yards or so to your shelter inside the tunnel beneath the bridge leading out of town. Join the hunched sleeping shapes there, the humid pulse of body heat. Just the one sentry on duty, ramshackle as you all are. A man who has insomnia. Gaunt. Biblical. Nods at you. Stares back out into the night. Still not quite enough to light a fire in the rusted barrel beside him.

Anything could happen, the closer to town you get. The closer to the factory. It's better living under the bridge. You would even if you had a choice, but that's probably a lie. The world beyond feels wrong. Infiltrated. The world beyond isn't really the world, would eat you alive given the chance. Not enough ways to know what's still out there, beyond the bridge.

The train's rare harsh call is half myth now. As rare as hearing an owl. Most of the owls have left, and the mice apparently loved the owls so much, they left too. Whatever "left" means. Nothing good.

It turns cold, like autumn nights used to be, the chill finally reaching you. The landscape having a dream of the past.

You cocoon into your little self-made corner, pile another dirty layer over yourself. Half hidden from the others by an overturned chest of drawers, a mound of plastic sheets, and molding clothes. Journal buried deep in the morass for now, until it's safe. Wary, you keep peeking out,

half expecting the creature to have followed you back to the tunnel.

You can't shake the image of the eyes in the water. That gaze.

<<**Demons** had lived in her town forever, staying to the shadows. But now they had come in numbers from another place. She was sure of it. **Demons** and drones, and who could tell the difference? Still she was left picking the worry spot on the back of her left hand bloody. Left picking at the feeling she would never be safe.

The **demons** favored any sort of shadow, slipped into view undercover. More and more took the form of strange men. People who looked like people, but were not. People who should belong, but didn't. Sometimes the new **demons** brought peculiar animals, on leashes. Animals that looked like dogs but didn't move like dogs, more like people crawling on all fours. Or with fur with odd reflective qualities, so that as they hunched past certain surfaces, they seemed to disappear.

If she talked about the **demons**, people thought she was crazy, because they already thought she was crazy because she was homeless. Or they'd pretend she hadn't said anything because they didn't want to think about it. But she knew better than anyone: She grew up here, if more as ghost than citizen. Too many disappearances, and with each, more gaps in the world. In memory.

Sometimes the **demons** appeared and other people ceased. That made her wonder if she had become delu-

sional. Or had been that way all along. Other times, anger: That others couldn't see what she saw. Or, worse, she wondered if they did see the **demons** but kept it to themselves.>>

- 6 -

Across the river, on the opposite bank, at dawn, out of mist . . . appears a pale, ethereal man. Angular. Skin so clear veins stand out like tributaries.

Framed by tangled forest and a rusted dead car sunk in the dirt, vines erupting from the carriage, and, beyond, the plumes from smokestacks of the factory. Smoke that curls into the sky above the tree line is not half so white as this man. His clothes glint or sheen or *move*. Catch what dappled light comes through the branches. He stands still, but not still, face so gaunt you can read it from afar. An intent that reads like search or journey.

He's not real to you. He's like a hallucination or a thought you had that's still inside your mind. Still far away. Until another like him appears beside him. Then he's real. Then, amplified, he frightens you.

You're hunched low and slunk. In the cool hollow of a berm overgrown with ferns. Wrens scold in the underbrush. Nothing else much moves or even seems to breathe. The two men are indistinct, wavering, through the bushes, as if they could move without moving. Or like you remain still but they're disappearing and reappearing again, in not quite the same place. Yet: the same place.

A sentinel quality, curled a bit like ferns as they survey the ground. Sense of a search. But they're not looking for you. Except they are. Because you have the journal. Because

you've seen the salamander. They just don't know who you are yet. Or who you might become.

When the third appears, bone-stark against forest greens, the pale man becomes unreal again. Suspended in the sunshine, in the glittering dust of his own stillness.

This third, the way he holds himself, the flicker of light on his eyes. You recognize pain when you see it, once you've plunged past the strangeness. They are sick, in pain. Reluctant, for that reason. But still they search, as if someone makes them search.

A smell of foul burning needles your nostrils, and you think they must be burning in the sun, melting, the mist or spray that reaches them. But then you realize it is just a new smell from the factory. The smell gains a weight and misdirection, like rusted iron soaked in honeysuckle. Devolves into a disgusting swill of hot asphalt and raw liver. With an aftertaste that is pungent. Makes it hard to tell the poison from the pain.

When the three pale men are roving distant again, you head back to the tunnel.

Midday. The others are out foraging, reflexive. Scouring what's empty or derelict. Names of the dead or those who moved on scrawled simple in black ballpoint on the opposite wall. A moment to assess yourself, to note new symptoms. The rasping cough won't go away. But won't kill you in the moment. Joint pain, headache, the same as always. Nothing beneath that. Not that you can detect. A collection of ills like pots and pans banging together in a jostling van.

You fool yourself that the river water is safe, but it's just safer than what comes out of the tap. Hunger pangs you ignore. Easy after years of it.

The fire in the barrel's gone out, cars hum and buzz across the bridge above. Sometimes drones take an interest, a different kind of buzz. The forest's a wall of green on the north end of the tunnel and burnt-out concrete blocks of a strip-mall office complex, heavily tagged, to the south. Just beyond, the dull walls of the main street, the gutters glaring with dirty runoff, the severe shadows, the shuttered doors and windows.

The journal's hidden good. Beneath a brick beneath a bag of dirty, rotting clothes, amid a pile of soft limestone soggy with water dripping down the underside of the bridge. Lines of lichen and sour gray mold disguise it. You imagine the journal vibrating with the energy of what it contains. You imagine the lichen and moss murmuring to it. Telling the journal to settle, to rest, to sleep. Drawing the demons out of it, to dissipate harmless in the air. But under brick it's cool and calm as if it's always been that way. Except for the fox, image like a secret blue sun pulsing at you underneath.

You're alert for the pale men, for discovery. But there's only an ancient porcupine noisy in the underbrush. Rustle of needles. No fruit to give him, but even polluted the forest must provide.

The journal still looks abandoned, not stolen. Pages singed by fire, some by rips made in anger. Curling at the edges. Stained. While something gulps and chortles from the river nearby, and you try to ignore that. The sound could mean anything or nothing. Heard the river enough

to know it changes, is never exactly one thing. Here, a toxic holding pond. There, a half-built muskrat lodge, home to some other critter.

Your sense of time has faded over the years, but probably you have thirty minutes, maybe an hour before the others return. Don't want them to think you have anything valuable. A long, hard lesson, that. Need and want were forces like demons.

Maybe it is an illusion of the charred pages, but the journal feels warm. Like it is really something else. Inside the journal, no name, no address. Unreturnable. Two marks that might be the letter C and the letter X or might not be.

Instead: Constellations or what you take to be constellations. Points of light with lines between them. Just a page or two. Each of the constellations is roughly circular. Notations in numbers beside each point. Smaller circles mapped to larger, as if the larger are replications that should show more details. But don't.

The first pages disturb you. Can't say why. There's something familiar about them. Maybe in the colors. Maybe in the shape of the door that pops up on page three. The door worries you. It makes you think of something opening that needed to stay shut. You imagine a vast darkness behind that door. Darkness you never want to know.

Then come diagrams of creatures that look like autopsies or recipes. Some almost whimsical: A plant that becomes a sea anemone that becomes a squid. Others like levels of hell. Bear-men and men like bears. Scenes of slaughter you pass quickly. More "instructions," in sentences and paragraphs written in a language you don't understand. Spanish in high school and some knowledge of Russian, so you

know other alphabets. But this matches nothing you've ever seen.

Page after page of this, until a few phrases in English. In a wild, uncontrolled handwriting, an alien language all its own. The English doesn't lead to anything useful, as if a trail of bread crumbs petered out into a sprawl of mushrooms or tiny black monoliths.

"The fox is reluctant, must be forced."

"Words coming to me remote from beyond the globes."

"No more Company."

Fair unfair: Most people living under the bridge over the years have been institutionalized, then released. Left to wander. True even in your childhood, or was what your parents told you to make you stay away from there. They share their writings sometimes, point at words and you nod and take them seriously, because it was serious, to them. Maybe the journal was a story of someone's life. Written in invented languages.

The journal mutters on most pages. Like someone muttering to himself, not writing to another person. Working out issues or equations or formulas. You don't know why you think the journal was written by a man, but you do.

The most disturbing images show mice being bred and re-bred to become smaller and smaller. In the last diagram, these new mice are being placed inside a person's throat, in an operation that cuts a hole in the throat. The human figure like the sexless figure in CPR instructions.

Some of the images in the journal remind you of the real world. A page has a thin figure on it like a druggie named Hal whose face had been cut up by a bottle in a

fight. He weighed all of ninety pounds. Probably didn't last the winter. Talked for hours about his former life. Husband. Homeowner. Programmer at a software firm. All that done now. But he kept reciting every detail for the three months you knew him.

You never talk about your past with anyone. Talking just releases memories into the air, and they aren't really yours anymore, or they become changed or other people capture them and hold them prisoner. You want to keep them. The bad ones might infect someone.

Scribbled in the margin, almost a plea or an order: *"You have to open your heart to as much as you can. As much as you can stand. No matter the cost."*

Such treacle. The sentiment is more surprising than finding sentences you can read. A few more like that, almost like greeting cards, until you wonder if it means something different. Wonder if this was some strategy for combating horror. But who created the horror? If you're reading this right.

"Everyone should have a magical garden. Everyone should know how that feels."

You skip and skim, unsettled, glance back at the fox from time to time. But he's no help.

Toward the end of the journal, you find sketches of a creature like what you glimpsed in the river. In a globe of light, like the fox on the cover. In a more scientific sense, carefully labeled, splayed, with eyes x'd out. A diagram. Resembles a salamander. A large salamander. Almost but not quite.

Like the languages you can't understand, the creature doesn't map to anything you've seen or read about. More

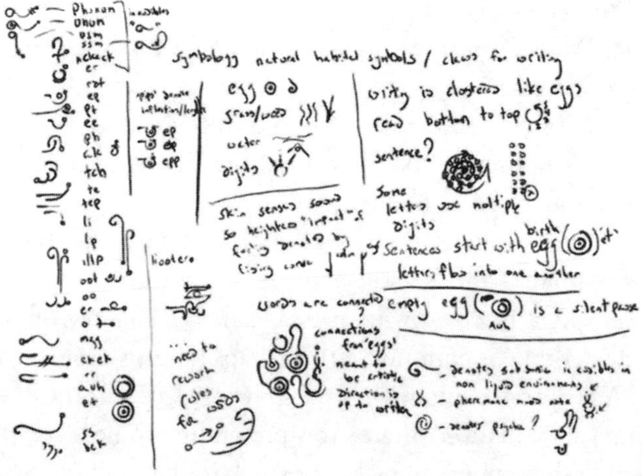

English, but only to support a delusion. A made-up language again. A salamander language?

Maybe you study that page for days, for months, for years. Maybe seconds. The page splits your brain into before and after. Becomes meaningless to gather meaning to it.

This page of a liquid language reminds you of pages from a book you were given, about the coast. In the surge of watery lines. The withdrawal at low tide, leaving spirals of tiny creatures behind. Husks and shadows and evidence of something hidden by the water, revealed.

Nothing like a eureka moment. Nothing except you know the others are coming back soon. So you memorize a simple phrase. What you think is a simple phrase, in salamander language. Put the journal back in its hiding place.

You go down to the riverbank, write in ephemeral, rich mud. Words, you think, or symbols. Of greeting. Of friendship. Of solidarity.

What if it is nonsense? Most days, all you have is reality, which is nonsense, too. The mud feels good against your hand. Soft and cool and forgiving.

Crouched there still when the drone appears on the opposite shore. Pain soars in your back, your arm. You squat lower, pivot to cover your message in the shadow of your body. A drone is common, but perhaps not this drone.

A beautiful thing with three glowing eyes, effortless as it comes close. Hovers there. You pretending to be a scrap of dead flesh propped up by bones stuck in the mud.

Who knows who sent the drone. Anyone could have sent it. Anyone could want anyone else gone. Evaporated in a millisecond. Never there. No scrap left to mark the human.

The drone sings to you for a while, querulous. A new thing you haven't seen before. It is half flesh, has wings like a hummingbird, a voice like a thrush or a wren, the carapace lithe plastic metal. Sings to you like an old friend. Craves a response. You know better.

But in the end, it doesn't want you. Or doesn't want you now. No demon sent it. Perhaps it's a surveyor. Perhaps there's no intent behind it at all. Anymore.

When the drone is gone, you shudder, relax, forage for food. Just another, ordinary day. Except you're convinced the factory is pretending now. Smoke is just to pretend it is still a factory, not something else. The drone came from that direction, you realize. Not the town. The three pale

men, they emerged from the side of the forest nearest the factory. Did they come from the factory? The smoke used to be invisible to you. Now it feels ominous, like portent.

You forage because your stomach is tight and small and aches. Berries will do. Orange mushrooms you know are safe, even if the forest stinks of gasoline half the time. As you search, the crisp blank pages beckon from the back of the journal like a kind of sustenance. Think on that as you bite down on sour berries to feel the seeds on your tongue. Your stomach hurts less. Mind becomes clear.

You decide to write on those pages. Things you cannot say aloud, that frighten you. Things you don't understand.

Now a door is opening. Now a world is coming in. Through the pages.

You know that already, but you don't know it yet.

<<**Demon** language was something the girl picked up from her evangelical mother—the last thing. The only thing retained. The meaningless words screamed or shouted or hissed or muttered as her mother stood over her bed at night. A bedtime story as the girl huddled under the covers until her mother had disgorged all the words, vomited them up until her brain was empty. The sound of her mother's uncut toenails against the wood floor was just like the dog they used to have.

Her mother thought the **demons** weren't just **demons** but retribution from God. Purposeful. Punishment. The girl, as she became a teenager, knew her mother was wrong, as she was wrong about so many things. Yet sometimes it

helped to think of them the way her mother talked about religion.

Whenever the girl wrote the word ***demon*** in those days, as in these, she felt compelled to use her own blood. As protection. As penance. Circles in her room. Shapes she found in books.

But what if the whole world was becoming a **demon**?>>

- 5 -

Some of the others ask too many questions once they spy the journal. Especially Eric, a gangly wreck who's newly arrived. Shock of the new. Thinks of homeless people as the kind of community they might be but aren't always. As separate from where he came from. And your eyes hurt from squinting in the poor light. You rebuff the questions even as you hide the journal deeper in your ragged blankets, your sleeping bag.

Huddled up against the side of the tunnel, in some dirt that is out of the wind. When Eric has become silent. When Eric is defeated. When Eric is staring out of the tunnel toward the river. Then you try to sleep again. One hand on the baseball bat. The sound of snow falling is from the journal, not from the world, but it's in your head regardless.

There is that cocoon of comfort in the journal. Some pages have the feel of summer. But others seem pulled out of the winter. The one that catches your eye cascades over two pages and captures the descent of a shooting star. Below, a creature made of darkness stares across a snowy plain at what may be the advancing claws and arms of some other monster entirely. All while splotches of snow fall, mixed with

the stars. Scrawled in the margin, another sketch of the fox head in a deep-sea-diver's helmet and words you can't understand.

At some point, or on another day, Eric's gone. People are gone. The tunnel lies abandoned. Except for the flotsam that is you. Losing track of time. Losing track of self. Do something practical to keep hold. Drive a stake into the ground. Not drift away into a dark pool. Resist a dive deep into the water. Commit to the now.

What've you got besides a mysterious journal? You take stock every morning, as if it might change. Because it might. You might have less. You can't afford less. A depressing inventory. A backpack, and inside a Walkman with a mixtape in it that skipped. From an old boyfriend, before you roamed so much. A sawed-off baseball bat. An antique lipstick case that was your mom's. Old bread you stole from a dumpster behind a grocery store. A can of tuna, but no can opener. A knife in your pants pocket for emergencies. A candy bar, also for emergencies. A gallon jug labeled "milk" filled with stream water.

A salamander, which hangs around, even as the weather cools. Message received, or not received. When you check the mud bank, there's just a swipe or swirl in response, the message gone.

A broken, polluted body.

Pale, unnatural men still creeping through the forest.

The salamander grows larger. Almost as you watch. Because you watch a lot. From underbrush. Behind trees. Peering around an empty barrel. You spy. You surveil. Waiting. For what? Drifting, receding, coming back into focus.

The salamander's shifting skin changed from green to red hot, the hazy sheen of a burning shed. The way of it, the weight of it, the patterns in the water. The feeling of being engulfed by a monster, yet not monstrous. Is there a map to lead you out of this? Or are you stuck?

You call it a salamander because that's all you know. From days as a kid getting lost in the woods and following the stream to get back. Always thought of them as slow, small, fragile.

But this creature in the river, this salamander, is so large now and churns the water, the swirls a teasing hint of its form.

But the eyes are perched on its head in a way unlike a salamander.

But it has serrated teeth.

But it has a tail with notches and fins to help stabilize it.

Can swim so fast it's here and then gone again. You watch it cut through the river, go deep then shallow, more like a shark might. The humid, close smell of the river fresh as the water parts. Fresher. Like it did once. Before there was a town.

It gets dark that day, but you can't stop watching. Belly full of thick dumplings made of cheap bread and a fifth of vodka someone left in an alley off of the main street. A test you either passed or failed. Let the demons in because the demons are already here. As some insect blinks and glows across the water and the salamander slides through, snuffs the light, brings it back again. A holy gloaming. Swiftness, the sharp intent . . . you don't have that. Maybe because you are not as new as this thing, or because you are not as new to this place.

Does it perform for you? Or is this just how it behaves? The salamander has no fear of you anymore. Has seen you run from the pale men. Seen you hide. Heard your low barked warning that one time, submerged before the pale men saw it. Warning that said, *We're on the same side of things.*

You tried speaking words to bring the salamander, in a rash moment. And then other words, with your finger in the water to form the words. Only to make it mad, smash its tail against the water and retreat. Then from the safety of the opposite bank reconsider you with those large, luminous eyes. Seemed to forgive you. *I know not what I say. I know not what to say.*

The salamander from safety opened its mouth and out came fluid singsong speech that covered and coated you. Soothed and lit a fire inside. Enraptured. The most beautiful, indescribable words ever heard.

Caught by that. Frightened by it.

Full retreat, quick strides back to the tunnel. Back to the wall, clutching a blanket like an old half-remembered stuffed toy. Heart pounding. Still feeling the embrace of that secret language. Feeling like the river runs into and through you. Out of your eyes your mouth. The salamander's message pouring out of you. So much information incoming to a receiver inadequate to receive it.

What does it mean, you want to know, what does it mean what does it mean even though there is meaning and there is the aching feeling that means your fate is linked to the salamander's.

You thought you would be the one to help the creature,

but you think the creature has to help you. Or you'll be lost. Among the demons. Among all the doors. For a moment you despair. Of all of it. The world. The world beyond. Your place in it. But that line in the water draws you back, the glide and the roll and dive of the thing you call salamander.

You still don't know what it calls itself.

Later, you feel an urge to see the salamander again. Leave your hiding place. Wander by obscure paths down to the riverbank. Moonlight makes shadows on the water, enough to see how smooth the water is, so devoid of ripples. Should you write another sentence in the mud? Maybe the salamander has left, gone far from here, followed the river down to the estuaries near the sea. Living a life you would love to live.

But no: A glimmer beneath the water, like submerged flame. The smell of dead leaves smoldering. The glimmer deepens, widens.

You leave another message in the mud. Subvert the intent, how your mother would write these things in greeting cards but mean the opposite.

Be safe. Be well. Be blessed.

<<**Demons** could come from the future to infect the past. **Demons** could take the form of giant fish to swallow her whole. **Demons** could speak to the dark. There was nothing wrong with the dark itself. She liked the dark for the way

it hid her and calmed her and cooled her. But **demons** became contaminated by it, drunk on it. **Demons** could forget to take any shape but just swallow the darkness and become darkness.

Demons lived in the abandoned factory now, as well as the City. Was it a punishment for the City? It wasn't clear.

In church, just the once, the girl's mother gave the sermon. No one knew except the girl, but the sermon was about her mother being mad at her stepfather for leaving. Or maybe some of the townsfolk guessed and didn't care.

The **demons** buzzed around her mother's head, disgorged themselves from the words coming out of her mouth, as if her mother's mouth were full of flies. Except it would have been better if they were just flies. And the not-flies burst into tiny flames and the flames became a shimmering face that roared out the words her mother merely said. Even though no one else noticed but sat in the pews frozen-smiling because although they saw no **demons**, they saw her mother and did not like what they saw.

The girl didn't tell her mother later, afraid of pills ground up into runny shepherd's pie or just another night of an argument she hadn't started.

The day she came home from school to find everything in her bathroom smashed or torn apart, in a mess her mother said she had to clean up. "The **demons** came," her mother said. "To punish you."

What was the difference between her family and **demons**? In truth, some **demons** were once people who did bad things even though they knew better. In truth, people

were **demons** when they didn't know any better. The girl had learned that it hardly mattered in the end.

Sometimes, the girl thought it was really her mother's name she should write in blood.>>

- 4 -

In the forest, at night, where the moonlight fades, you glimpse the darkness moving. Emerging from the factory, the factory opening up like a maw in your head that devours all.

Coming closer to the bridge, to the tunnel. Everything around it is so still you know it's not your imagination. Drift and glide, the way the motion feels like the brush of a dark wing then like a monstrous head eclipsing the shadows of branches. Faint sound of a deliberate pace, on two legs not four.

How as you hide in the rags and ruin of an old sleeping bag. How as you pretend to be dead, to be nothing human. As you stare through a veil of dirty white cloth at the pale dark of the underside of the bridge.

That is when it comes close, disguised by stealth. Veiled, it is a shape made of parts that don't fit. Lithe and ponderous. Thin yet thick. Reptilian yet birdlike. But an eye so sharp, letting so much light in, you can feel its gaze pulling at the edges of you. Pulling at you like it means to unravel you. Tugging. Teasing.

Don't you want to be revealed? Don't you?

There comes a smell that's antiseptic yet fresh with blood. There comes a smell like a questing all its own, like

senses for this *thing* mean something different than they mean for you. That it might never see you, and yet know you entire. Devour you. Entire. The tunnel bricked-up.

You feel buried. Suffocating.

Never see the light, be forever staring up into nothing and nowhere.

Many creatures in the forest have become nocturnal. You tell yourself as the monster comes close. Faded into night because day is too dangerous. As you shut down. A homeless man told you. A biologist. Laid off. Discredited. By a pipeline company. The man rambled like he'd rambled on hikes, across wilderness he loved that only existed now in his mind. Then he'd disappeared. But from him you knew porcupines loved fruit. That maybe a fox, even a blue fox, could creep through the day as well as the dark.

Pulsating, kinetic, imbued with something twinned to the life you have now—how something inside you knows more than you do. It knows the future. It can see a few moves ahead, even if you can't do anything about what happens. Like, you'd only seen the one pale man in your dreams, and he'd been falling into a bed of roses that became snow globes that became a myriad of worlds. And in every one of those worlds there was a burning shed and a pale man on the opposite shore and you can't remember if you had the dream before or after you saw the pale men.

Parts of the journal, when you take it out again at dawn, in that curious gray light that wants to leave you guessing as to whether the world is beginning or ending . . . why those parts are familiar. For the demon creature takes many forms in the journal. Sometimes he is cadaverous and seems trapped in an agony of self-doubt. In one sketch, he lives inside an alchemical bubble of air and water protected by a swirling wall of dust and sand. A kind of soft outer shell. Like something waiting to be born. In some, he reflects the somber mask of a bat. Trying out roles.

To calm yourself from the onslaught, you tell the ferns and the dirt what you know to be true, the children's story your mother told you once, and then ever after only with bile, with sarcasm, so you've had to change it. She always said you were still a child to believe in it.

This was the story: Over all the forest beyond their home and the little shed, over all of it. Over all. Ruled the forest mind. Which seemed to slumber and not remember and be simple. To be made of earth and trees and clouds and birds. But was actually awake in a way no person could be awake. Slumber that was not sleep. Mind that was not mind. A person could never imprison that mind, only destroy parts of it, bit by bit. But as long as even a small piece remained, it could never die. Would never die.

Might save you to save itself or, in the end, might not even notice you small and huddled against the wall of a tunnel.

When it's gone. Crept past the tunnel mouth. Receded into the forest. When you cannot feel that awful weight. When, hours later, the tickle and itch of sun at the edges brings a different kind of heat and you're sweating. The eye of the monster that will grow in dreams, red and swollen and dark.

Then you remove the veil. Sit up on your elbows. Release your breath. Scream and scream until you're hoarse at what it left behind.

The pale man's head staring sightless up at you from the ground.

The tunnel feels like the maw of a giant fish. Devoured. Digested. Broken down for parts. Nothing human. Nothing real, flesh-and-blood. Just a witness to atrocity. Your mind on fire, and nothing to put it out. You cannot move, cannot speak. Don't know where to look for something that might calm your raging pulse, the ringing in your ears. The way the world tilts and shifts.

Smell the clean rasp of water alive with so many things.

On the tunnel wall, the salamander appears like magic. Like mimicry and camouflage. Skin hue turning from dirty white and wall-textured to a humming orange tinged with green. Strobing gentle.

Was it always there? Watching?

Becomes horizontal, walking up to you. Still you can't move. Broad bullet of that head, now almost larger than you, the muscular body behind it, the curling question of the thick tail.

The salamander's eyes gulp, spin, recover in the wet drawl of pupil split vertically and come back together. Staring at you, and you, finally, unable to look away. The hue changes

in the moment. From violet to aquamarine to pink and then into the most spectacular shade of light blue. Shifts again.

Rough, soft pad of toes against your arm a good sign. Trust, too, in how you do not flinch, pull away. Read once that salamanders can be poisoned by touch. How any oil or soap, any unnatural thing can hurt them. That you can hurt by touch. That you can hurt another living being just by existing in the world. Just by passing through the world. That is all. That is all. Panic, wanting to pull away, to preserve, to avoid causing distress.

But the touch is steady, warm, insistent. Reassures though you do not want to be reassured, know that keeping the horror of what happened in your mind is survival. Don't want to hurt to feel. Don't want to remember. Can't get past it. Into the future. There's nothing that cannot be reconciled, the salamander's gaze tells you. Caught in that gaze, in the touch. A wall of globes that causes pain.

Then the salamander is gone, taking the pale man's eyeless head with it. Still feel the touch. The touch exists all around you. Makes the world better. Takes part of your past with him.

Back in the forest, you see from afar two pale men searching for their third. Hear the distant cry of their distress, the call inhuman that is the flare sent up for their brother. It sounds like the caw of a crow hiss-mumbled so it tumbles out into the world ungainly and new.

In the journal, the pale men and the dark bird are on the same page. But here, in this forest, they are enemies.

<<The **demons** always came out at night. Certain incarnations had a grin on their faces, even when they meant to do harm. That was worse than being a true monster, because true monsters didn't first try to be a friend. And the worst thing was, people wanted to be fooled even as they knew they were being charmed. Even when they knew what was coming. Even when the girl knew what the smile might turn into. The reflection of the moon in their eyes became a kind of juddering cruel laugh and then the rush, the enveloping.

Demons could speak to the dark. But **demons** became contaminated by it, and that's why they couldn't be trusted. A **demon** that couldn't be trusted was a terrible thing. Then she couldn't predict what it might do. Which is why when she grew up, she gave up alcohol unless it was the only thing she had to drink. Alcohol made it hard to tell a **demon** from a monster.

But in truth . . . the truth about **demons** was primal, awful, chaotic darkness with a will and an evil smile and eyes that were everywhere, torn holes not pinpricks, that saw through her or saw into her and crushed her marrow and froze her brain and collapsed her spine and made her piss in her pants. Nothing kind or gentle or wise. Why should **demons** have to be, when they were used to having their way?

These thoughts came back to her as an adult, as she watched, hidden, as **demons** poured out of the abandoned factory, eager to infect the world. To conquer it. If they looked like people, who would know the difference? If they weren't the same **demons** as before, did it matter?>>

They are taken too far out of you. They're too distant now. All the things you could have done. There's only where you are now. With the world closing in. Hunting you, and you become wraith, phantom, a mere notion and a smudge of night.

The next week, you visit the soup kitchen in town. But now it feels odd, like you don't belong. Vision green-tinged for a time. A film you blame on the rain, and what might live in the rain. But you can't be sure. Too many strangers. Too many factory workers who stare around them as if looking for something. You distrusted them already, for what they did. But now you distrust them for who they might be.

No one lives in the tunnel now except you. Where did they go? Where could they go? But you couldn't follow, despite the danger. You couldn't because of the salamander. Even with the pale men and the dark bird searching. The pale men have grown in number and then receded, as the dark bird kills them. Does it kill them because they failed or because they are sick?

You found the drone crumpled, spilling blood from a jagged gash, antennae still twitching. Nothing you could do for it, not even to risk killing it to kill its pain. Splayed out in a forest clearing like bait. No more drones will come, and that frightens you as once the drone frightened you. It means whatever the invasion is . . . it's winning.

You hide the journal in a different place every day. Every night. Sneak glances at its pages as if it might give up its mysteries. But more that it might help you know what to do.

A dark, reptilian bird smudged like ash on one page. Dark and twisted. Hard to read. Sketches and a smattering of words you understand. A fable. Of a cruel father. Of a boy whose sanctuary had been turned into a hell.

A word you think is English, *Nocturnalia*, sketches that look like a reverie become dangerous. Creatures losing their minds. Swiggles and arrows like particles carried through the air. Nerve gas? Pollutant? But intentional. Some miasma in the air that makes creatures behave odd. Invisible. Or maybe you're wrong and it describes something else.

No help at all.

You spend more time in a hidden hollow in the forest. Surrounded by the moss and lichen and pine straw. The soft cool spring of loam beneath your body. The forest mind running through the forest floor. Suppressing your cough. Staring up at the canopy, the woodpeckers and jays and warblers that stitch their way between. Waiting for the sound of the pale men. Waiting for the sound of the dark bird. Death seems like a dream, a puzzle you cannot solve. What will death be like in this maze?

Then the salamander creeps close and looks down into your hollow. Makes a low burbling sound. Turns to look back over its shoulder. Burbles again, facing you.

You don't understand.

The salamander throws up all over you. Shock. Then, calm.

A light pink liquid, in that light, which seeps everywhere, holds you in place from surprise and some hidden quality you can't describe. The liquid cools you. Feels like nothing. Feels like air throbbing against you, thickening and thinning

to form-fit you. Smooth comfort. Spreading across your arms and your legs, and any reason to move fades from you.

You laugh, delighted. It smells of bubble gum. The smell of watermelon bubble gum! Which you used to buy when you could afford it. Chew it like food for hours. Fool the stomach.

Again, the salamander vomits, this time over itself, and you see the pink surround it, coursing like an organism. Traveling with purpose. Through the glaze across your eyes. The breathing through your skin that is not your skin. The salamander slides in beside you. A solid, a hefty weight. Its belly is distended as if full of young. Tight fit, and you now looking into its eyes as you both wait for the next thing.

Down in the pit of the hollow, so close to something so alien.

A shadow rises across the lip of the hollow. A familiar shape. The dark bird, the reptilian smirk of beak, the bloodshot eye you can imagine despite the dark. But you cannot even tense up against your second skin. Which breathes for you now as if you are covered in lungs or gills, feeding your body through the skin.

The dark bird stares down into the hollow. The dark bird stares for a long time. You and the salamander are so very still, so very close. Your mind roams, passing through the eye of the salamander and into a world of ripple and wave of endless floating and quick darting motion. Weaving through weeds and bulrushes and over cool stones at the bottom of the river. The thrill of liquid against the body, the constraint of that. The way it reminds you the world matters in a way that breathing air cannot.

The dark bird cannot see you. You're under the river, scouring the bottom. So very far away from the hollow.

Comes the snarl, an expression of frustration or bloodlust. The dark bird falls away from the edge of the hollow. The shadow relaxes into normal night.

After, you and the salamander wash off in the river, watch as a thin scrim in the shape of you, of the salamander, floats downstream. Faintly luminous. Dissolving.

The salamander writes something in the water. It disappears, then widens. Just exists in your memory, as if you are at the center of the ripples. As if you're diving through the calm of the center into deep water. As if you are monstrous.

"I don't understand," you whisper.

But you do.

Your blood is different now. The salamander has done something to it. You feel rejuvenated somehow, even with smell of gasoline lingering in the wind.

The salamander burbles at you once, twice, then, ponderous and huge, plunges into the river and is gone.

When you write the word *demon* in the journal, it means something different. It's like the blood snuffs out what the word means. But, also, there is something peering out from the page that wasn't there before.

Some part of the salamander lives in the journal now.

You've never begrudged your maker the daily pain, the lack of comfort. Lack of care. The cold. The heat. The things you have to do. It isn't easy, but it isn't hard, either. Because

you have to. The way you live. You can't remember another way. You can't forget.

Does it matter to the forests or the smokestacks or the sky? Does it matter to the salamander or the strange pale men or the mice in their meadow, the deer in their field? Does it matter to the course of the river or the street or how the town expands or contracts or fills up with drones? Does it matter?

You don't know where to look now, after the encounter with the salamander. You don't know what to do. The eye of the salamander confronts you. Challenges you. The words it spoke to you in the language you'll never understand. You can never ask it what it wants or what it needs. All you can do is try to understand what exists in the body. Try to feel what it's like to live in water. What it means for a body to communicate with the world so intensely, so directly, for the world to be so up against you that you and it are the same thing.

If you're born to it, if you're like the salamander, it must be like heaven, as if heaven were on Earth. The hell must be that no one will leave you alone here in heaven. That people hunt you and people kill you and people just cannot be still in their own bodies and listen and watch and hear but must somehow escape the beat of their own hearts by ever being in motion, even when they come to rest.

As you have come to rest, frozen, pinned by the intent in the salamander's gaze. There is prophecy there. What it means. How it means. Why it means. When it is meant.

As you write in the journal, the pain is less. Your headache is gone. Your rash is gone.

<<Her past happened to another person. Another girl. Drab, dull, ordinary. She thinks of it as a fairy tale with no point. Once, as a child, she had lived in a cottage at the edge of town, in sight of the smokestacks. With her mom and her stepdad, this girl she was.

Even then, she'd known there was something in the house, something under the house, just could not put a name to it. Depending on her mood it was benign or horrible. But it was always the thing under the house that caused the arguments between her parents. It was the thing under the house that made her real father leave.

After a while, she became convinced the thing under the house had come up through a tunnel and into her brain. When she told her mother, before the idea infected her mother, the man at the hospital with the glittering water-faucet smile told her that wasn't true. She didn't believe him. Why else would her mother keep arguing even after her stepfather had left? Why else would there be another voice in the girl's head?

The girl's real father had left at birth, all that remained a few toys bought at a dollar store near the honky-tonk a few miles down the road. Where he'd met her mother before she got fired and went to work in fast food. She didn't want to like any of those toys, but she was fond of a plastic boat her mom called "the ark," but she just called Boat.

When the girl's stepfather saw Boat, he told her that he had owned a boat once and lived on the coast. When he wasn't drunk, he'd told her stories about the tidal pools and wandering at sunset between them, and the treasures found

there. He'd shown her photographs and pictures in books. Like he wanted his past to become her future.

The girl would never see the ocean. It was too far away from town. Too far away from the tunnel that became her home. But she did remember playing with Boat in the bathtub, and taking her toys and plastic jewelry and creating tidal pools to explore. She had an active imagination. Her mother always said. Sometimes spat the words. Sometimes punished her for it. Which was when it was important to focus on the sea and the day when she might live in a little cottage on the shore.

Her stepfather's stories weren't much, but they meant almost too much to the girl. She knew it, but couldn't help it.

Once, in a rare bout of kindness, the day after her stepfather left them, her **mother** had made star-and-moon mobiles to hang off the showerhead, and the girl had piloted Boat across the sea of the tub by the light of those stars.

That was when the dark began to take form, shape in her mind, and she began to call what lived in the **house** and lurked in the **town** what they really were: **demons**.>>

– 2 –

That night. Which night. *That* one. Or that one. You're losing track. Of time. Of symptoms. Of the world. But, *that* night, the dark came down and killed a pale man—and then another. Drags them off toward the factory smokestacks. Sound of their bodies through underbrush silky, smooth, disturbing, as if they move like molting snakes down a soft carpet. But

the thing that drags them is rough, harsh, cracked branches and the night does not matter to it. Forces in the world that seem so mysterious are at odds. That it is not dark against light but dark against dark against dark against dark.

Charting the English words through the journal, stitching them together into sense or a kind of sense. Thinking it gives you an anchor, even as each sets you more adrift.

"What if the world were alive, the entire world, every thing in it. What if I could make that world, and each being connected in such intimate ways."

So dark, too, in the tunnel you venture from, the way its voices are so silent. Realize at some point that the others were as scared of you as the thing that drags the corpses of pale men through the forest.

"What men make of the future must be better than the past. If the world is to live, we must make better things."

There, in the twilight, too, you imagine the salamander, hidden away against tree roots at the riverbank. The salamander, safe in subterranean hollows, in murky water, in among the river grasses, the algae and smooth rocks. While, above, the last pale man runs for safety, across the meadow and the fields and the forest. The dark bird following swift, close on the scent, and you realize the sound of it dragging its murdered burden comes to you from the past.

"I cannot see the destination sometimes. But I know the work must continue. 10, 7, 3, 0."

The sound of the bird and the blood-red eyes and a sulfur smell and a scream and one will must win out. Another pale man has died. You imagine talons ripping through

translucent skin, toward the visible heart beating its last. Delicate as a tree frog. Not up to the challenge.

"I search for it in entrails and in skulls. I must believe that it lives there."

You find the damp part of the forest, where the moss is joined by the ferns and the ground curves down and water trickles continual. Where black iridescent damselflies glide and flit, still, then in the air again. Like something that could be torn apart in an instant, crumpled and thrown aside as if it had never existed. Find the places where the rotted wood of fallen trees gives shelter. Burrow deep like a fox. Hide your pack. Place the journal in a used plastic baggie, bury it in loam far from your hiding place. Until the next time.

The writing has come slower and slower, as you feel compelled to use blood for more and more of the words. But still you keep at it. A vague sense of needing a record. Something the salamander said to you. About commitment. About escape or no escape and there might come a time when it could not protect you. Or you think it said this. There have been too many demons to concentrate, to know for sure.

You love the soil against your skin. You love the water against your skin, the forest a kind of bliss. Or perhaps it is only that the salamander loves these things. Does it matter? The places covered in comforting dead leaves. The loam and the lichen, the earthworms and the snails, the mushrooms and the mold. Fungi like lampposts or markers illuminating the world. When you write in the journal, it feels like your skin is open to the messages it sends out, the messages you embed there. How these places, too, are tidal pools, the forest an island amid devastation.

The glow at night, of fireflies and, overhead, the canopy and the moon and, even, you imagine, a fox staring down at you, framed by leaves and dark branches. The face of a fox impassive, remote, centuries away. So far away. As far away as the moon.

Later. You fell asleep or fell awake. In the night, deep into it, so little difference, so little defense. But the forest now is full of light. Waves of red flickering light in a rough line, and a figure, distant, at the center of the line. Coming closer and closer across the shadows of tree trunks. No difference between flame and figure, as if the figure is made of light and holding out infinite arms of fire. But there is no smell of burning. But there is no crackling or hissing sound. Just the muffled sound of someone walking over damp leaves and branches.

Your mother. From your shelter, peering over a fallen log, you see that the figure is your mother. A burning flame, setting fire to the forest with the fury and derangement of her passage. Reaching out with blackened hands, the flame now wings to her sides. Beseeching. Imploring. You can hear her now, above the silence of the flames. Calling out your name. Asking you to help, to stop the pain. To stop hiding.

What's the present but a version of the past. You piss yourself with fear. Your heartbeat pulses strong in your ears as if the pressure has dropped. Pass out. Recover. Come to your senses, lurching onto your stomach, still hidden. But not for long. She is near. She is so close.

The fine-etched features of your mother's face, so locked

in. As if set on a course for too many years, and even though the destination never appeared, still she must continue toward it, through a field of flame. Must find her daughter. To explain? To inflict? But that is only your fear rising again.

The fire is hypnotic. The fire calls your name, too. Fire and mother both. You cannot run. You cannot reveal yourself.

Until your mother stands on the lip of your shelter and stares down at you, her green velvet nightgown on fire and her eyes like raging candles.

The hand she extends toward you is the edge of a dark, dark wing amid the burning loose fabric of her sleeve. Her face has turned reptilian and alien and talons clamp onto your shoulder and you're lost. Lost, never to be found. Lost and no saving you should you burrow among the grubs and the moles and the other creatures hidden beneath the forest floor.

Frantic, you push away, try to rise, trip, fall back against the opposite side of the hollow, tree roots holding you up. Knives slice into your shoulder, how blood trickles out and the talons come in for another strike. The dark wing stands there, red eyes hungry. It will flay you alive, take your soul. Use you up as demons do.

That's when the salamander barrels out of the dark, so much larger than before, smashes thrashing into the dark wing, and they fall, struggling, silent, terrible monsters, back into the darkness.

The moment you can move again. Find the journal. Pick up your pack. Run.

<<Her stepfather used to creep around the cottage as if a lurker, a stealthy walker, a shadow, a wraith. He would leave framed photos of his family on the walls to mark his territory, but he himself often seemed invisible. Then wasn't there anymore, taken by **demons**.

Once her **mother** explained that he was mostly a ghost because "He doesn't want to do harm." But she knew that wasn't true. Maybe it just made everything easier for him. Did ghosts have shouting matches with her **mother** in the bedroom with the door closed? And when he was gone, all that remained were tidal pools in the girl's head and the portraits to show that, once, he had hung something on the wall.

His absence opened up a hole in her life she hadn't known was there. As if he'd been an eclipse and the first abandonment now shone forth in all its heat and glory. The father she'd never known, who had never been in her life and about whom her **mother** said only vague things, like, "He was a good man," or "He did like his sports," as if any of it couldn't describe a thousand men. Had he really been so ordinary?

Worse, alone with her **mother** . . . her **mother** was still the same—the woman with the pinched cheeks and mussed-up blond hair who tried hard most of the time, but would just as easily fill her cereal bowl with orange juice as milk, and when she complained would find a way to blame her.

Mother said she had no photos of the girl's real dad. But once the girl went through some drawers looking to borrow a pair of her **mother**'s socks and found an envelope of old black-and-white photos of stern-looking **people** with narrow, pinched features and severe, sharp black clothes. She

knew they weren't their family or her stepdad's family. They looked like no one she would ever have wanted to meet. They looked, upon reflection, in their reflections, like **demons**. As stiff and pale as the **demons** she watched become the town.

Not long after, her **mother** slammed open the girl's door, breathless, shouting: "You did it! You did. You're the **demon**. He left because you're a **demon**. I wish you'd never been born!"

In the morning, her **mother** becoming **Other** had forgotten bursting in, forgotten that her **daughter** was a **demon**. But the girl remembered.>>

- 1 -

The dark bird cries out in pain, lost in the forest, wing useless from the salamander's attack. Cries of alarm distant from the factory, as if the dark wing is a beacon. From your place by the river, beside the salamander, who is changing again. Not from wounding but from choice, from life cycle. That much you understand.

The huge body beside you, engulfed by a river grown urgent, tugs at the creature. Tugs away at the strings, the knots of its body. As you watch, the salamander begins to disintegrate, the tail becoming a slow miracle of thousands of tiny writhing salamanders where one had been.

The limbs and torso fall like living red sand into the river, taken by the swirls. Until there is only the head and the eyes that stare at you, until the erosion of self takes them too, and it all crumbles into the water and the river is awash with motes of life.

Such joy in the sight. So much joy you feel that the pain leaves you for a time. To see a river that is full of wriggling red bodies. Tiny eyes so bright, staring as one at you, and then swept downriver. Changing the river, changing this world. A river aflame. Dispersed and disbanded and yet ever stronger in that fragmented state.

And the thing you didn't know at first: The dark bird is coming closer. You've lost a lot of blood, the wound too deep, too poisoned for the salamander to repair. Not and save itself. But it has a plan, a plan it whispered to you. A plan you're willing to accept.

Nothing left to do. Nothing you can do. For what could you do. This has all already happened.

<<A hot spring day, the leaves dying on the trees and no one could guess that **they** were the reason. The girl came home from school, walked to the back porch, found her mother there, pacing, agitated.

There was no warning. There seemed to be no motive. Perhaps it was a poison skimming the mind, present in the blood. Perhaps it was some pent-up rage that fell upon her **Other** for little reason. Perhaps perhaps perhaps.

"The **demons are in the shed," her Other** told her. "The **demons** are trapped in the shed. I trapped them. Pour the gasoline. Pour it. Make a bonfire. Kill the **demons**. Kill them!" Red reptilian eyes, but the girl only saw that it would get worse if she didn't.

So the girl took the cans of gasoline down to the shed, poured them on the wood. It was a little shed with nothing

in it except the **demons**. Dirt all around. What harm could it do to burn it down, the girl reasoned. If it would calm her **Other**. If maybe she could have an evening of peace or something like it.

The smell was harsh as her **Other**'s voice, so she hurried for the match, to smell something different. The shed lit up brilliant, with a gasp, gush, and shallow scream. The flames traveled up to the roof in seconds. It was always brittle and dry and rotted. Diseased.

The scream of fire became a human scream, but by then it was too late. While her **Other** laughed and danced beside the girl and shrieked out, "He came back! He came back! But he was a **demon**! But he was a **demon**! So I gagged him! So I tied him up!"

The shed on fire. The shed extinguished, blackened, strewn with ash.

The girl's stepfather is inside. The girl's stepfather is not inside. Her **Other** put him there. Her **Other** did not put him there. If the girl doesn't look inside, she can make the reality she wants to live in, the one that won't make her scream. The one that won't mean she spends time in a juvenile detention center. Becomes an old, old high-school dropout. Never stable. Even her **Other** and the **demons** become dull, predictable, fuzzy, lost behind a veil, and even that is a sort of loss.

Never able to recover because how could she recover from that?

Thinking: Perhaps the hot spring day, harbinger, had deranged both of them. If the world was a **demon** that wanted to kill everyone, what did it matter? Did her **Other** know

something true, in her body? Did she burn him in the shed because she knew what was coming and she wasn't the equal of it? To survive the death of the world? If she wanted to die, she could have chosen some other way.

Nocturnalia. Nocturnalia. Nocturnalia. The giant fish diving, diving deep, lingering in the depths beneath her. Waiting to devour her. Or had devoured her. Or would have.

In prison terrible things happened to her and she didn't care. For a long time, she didn't care. For a long time, she thought the **demons** died with her **Other**, short months later.

At least she hadn't lived to see her daughter huddled in a tunnel under a bridge, poring madly over a journal that could not possibly, it was not possible, carry meaning. Could mean nothing to no one.

A shed and a fire but no one really in there or that the body they did find had been someone else.

She knew only the marker of territory who, like a fox, didn't want to be seen, but only to be.**>>**

- 0 -

Things that can be said. Things that can't be said. You know them both. Still the smokestacks belch smoke. Still you tunnel under the bridge, you will never be quit of the place. You will never be quit. You will live always, even when you don't. You will never have the right to decide or to understand. You will only have the right to help or not help. Through all the versions. Yourself. Not yourself.

Darkness encroaches from across the river and the salamander is truly gone and the river is calm once more.

Darkness behind and above the tunnel, on the bridge, there stands the shadow of a fox. At the end of the tunnel, a vision you know must be false, but is still better than darkness: A shining City surrounded by gardens and streams. Surrounded by a swirl of snow that forms a portal, a window, almost a globe of light. Nothing else to do but to come closer, the dark bird in pursuit. The City ahead, the City you recognize.

It's snowing all around as you walk into that vision. It's snowing and you feel the soft, shadowy breath, the baleful stare of eye. But you are not afraid. You are not afraid. That, at least, the salamander has given you. Or you have taken it.

You step into the tunnel, into the snow. A sense of a weight lifting from you and you're through the tunnel, through the window, and come out gasping into a desert City, the snow still falling, like a miracle, except now you see it's ash and the Company building is aflame and around you lies the shattered bulk of a vast leviathan.

There's a ravine of blackened trees that shouldn't be there, a ruined City that shouldn't be there. You stumble down to the polluted river past the Balcony Cliffs. You stumble down, falling, struggling in the mud. Pick yourself back up.

And there shall be a wall of globes. And there shall be a man with mice in his throat. A dark bird about to take you apart and no one there to stop it. Only to watch. The strange man says your name, and the word is terrifying in his mouth. "You shouldn't have done this. You shouldn't have taken the journal." Nods to dark birds. Nods to the men standing behind him. Swarming now. Merciless now.

But the salamander's there, too, at the edge of the river in your mind. And you give yourself over to him. And he envelops you and in that cool embrace, in that moment where his skin is breathing into you. Speaking to you in that unbearably beautiful language, that unknown, unknowable language. Unfathomable and fathoms deep.

Such a great and abiding light and an orchestral majesty to the invisible molecules of the air.

In that moment, the salamander takes everything from you, before they can. All of it. Every last thing. All the poison and the need, the imperfections and the want. The incurable wound, the things that make you human but hold you back. Gives them to the ones who are killing you now. To the ones who deserve it.

Neither of you will be the same again. Neither can ever be the same again. Both are different and in different ways. And yet, in the moment, on the long journey ahead, recognized. Not alone. Never alone.

You'll never be part of history. But you'll carry history with you. And even though you don't really escape until much later. Even though you know what's really happened to you, he's there. Makes you free. Makes you ready.

For the next thing.

<<The girl's name was Sarah. She didn't mean to travel so far, for so long, or to become so different. She didn't mean to become a **demon**.>>

7. CORPSE

v.5.09

Once, there had been no Company upon that desert plain. Once, there had been no City. Only a river running clear and clean. Only the fringe of green around its banks, the birds overhead, the creatures of the land that inhabited that place. A vast plain of reeds and grass, through which passed multitudes.

The first fish of Behemoth's kind had come out of that river. Had sat there on the mud flats breathing in and breathing out as the dawn light heated the ground, water rose through the mud. And from that first fish had come the next, and the next, and they had grown in size and number, eaten and been eaten. Herons had stalked them and they had stalked little frogs and crabs.

Some of Behemoth's kind grew leviathan-large and walked across the land in search of food before returning to the sanctuary of the river. The area of plains at the edge of what would become the City flooded and left behind bogs and ponds and this brought damselflies and other creatures that had not been there before. Reproduced. Lived long lives.

Burst forth: from a clutch of soft transparent eggs. Burst forth: from tethering to the bottom of a reed in a swollen river. Behemoth burst forth and swam to the river's bank and looked out upon the City in its infancy, across a field of holding ponds that would one day become a desert.

Burst forth: What am I? What am I? How am I connected? What is my purpose? What is all of this, felt in the flesh? Why is it so beautiful? What is beautiful? Why do I not know? What else don't I know? When will I know it? Will I ever know? Would knowing be too much?

burst forth: behemoth tiny evaded toad and frog to scuttle-crawl between holding ponds / flop-plopped into water deft of fin / mud clear as bright sun / cavorted with others of his kind / until absent / devoured in clutches / in mid-dart solitary / until there was only behemoth / aquiver in the mud / alert for the crux / of enrapturing jaws / that one day behemoth would repeat

throb on a cusp of reed, clutch water-lily stalks / cling hidden against / the drift warp / of swirling thick water / infinitesimal on the edge / of the infinite.

sudden convulsion of faith, of belief / behemoth had never truly been alone / not with so many allies in earth, sky, and water / that was not emptiness / that was not the stars bounded by nothing / and below / across a dark plain / a building that burned and never turned to ash / a heart that beat and never died

behemoth satisfied by the sun upon a muddy rock / watched the stitching of black damselflies over the bog / so little sound leaking from their wings / how the delicate tracery escaped / negated all behemoth would ever be / even small / even staring into a bridge tunnel, damselfly like a drone hovering in the air / hovering in the sky / hovering in dreams

the last of the green

Escaping from Behemoth as he lay wheezing or still, or both, across some length of broken expanse. The sky was now like staring up at the gray-silver surface of a holding pond from its depth. Escaping Behemoth. Out across the ground. Taking part of Behemoth away, leaving what it could.

Taking all that she could, because one day there would be no Company building, no City.

Burst forth: Did you ever need to live on as I needed you to live on? Did you ever have a need so great that the vestiges of your mission existed even if you weren't sure you did? Did you ever believe you were a ghost? Did you ever reach a point when you weren't sure purpose existed anymore? And yet, still, you were here.

Until in the thinning and the thrashing there came a silence, and Behemoth realized it was the silence. It was the silence. It was the stillness. Nothing moved but the wind. Nothing moved but the scavengers of the holding pond, come to observe, to take what could be taken. Peered scared. But all that was left was the stillness.

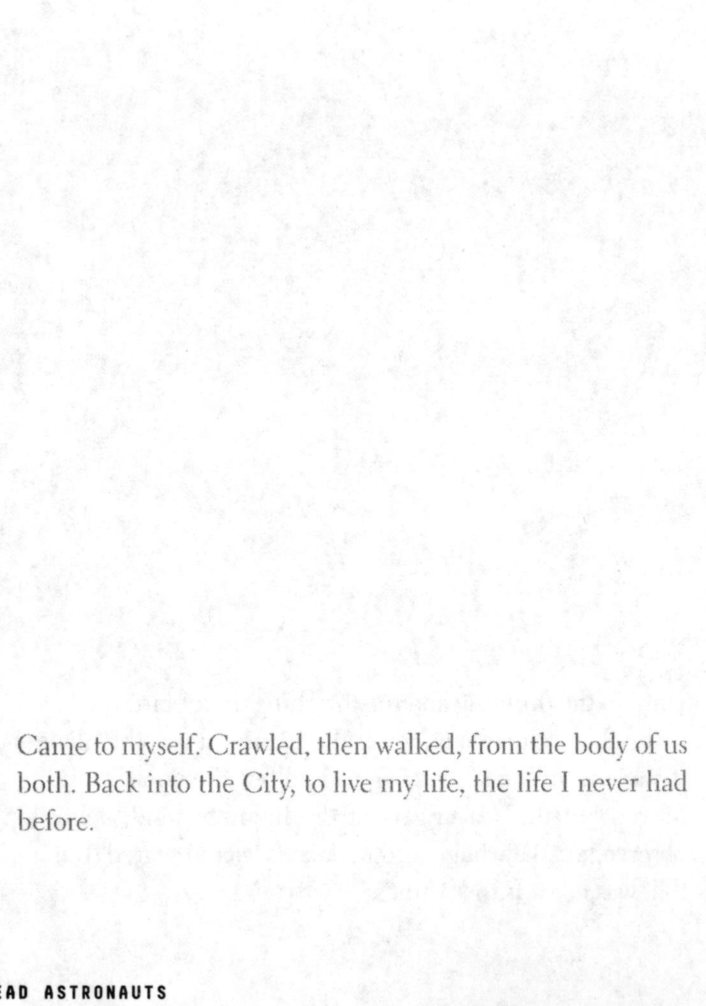

Came to myself. Crawled, then walked, from the body of us both. Back into the City, to live my life, the life I never had before.

The great carcass lay beside the Company building. It stank for days. The flesh crumbled in on itself. Flaked and rancid. Many fed for months. Even on the dried, weathered flesh. Even on the network of scars. Until even the scars were gone and then the bones and then all trace.

Neither was the same again. Neither could ever be the same again. Both were different and in different ways. And, yet, in the moment, on the long journey ahead: Recognized. Not alone. Never alone.

That blue and verdant lake of youth. The blazing, blinding blue reflects. Can't remember. Can't forget. Hops to the water's surface, wary of herons. Peers out through the reeds once more and forever.

Dives in.

Gone.

Not gone.

8. THE DARK BIRD

v.4.2

Murder control not quite gone, through all the haze of sand and fog, the breath of wind and the breeze curling unruly over dead river, half-dead City. Murder control clicking like a switch flipped like a click like a cut like a blood-covered switch that clicked on, beckoned, beaconed off. Bodies, the memories of bodies all along that blasted plain, rendered down to coordinates, stashed away like caches, but only in memory or abandoned museums. Except memory was murder control.

Faces limned by the beatific cowl of sea salt and crumbling fossils. The dried black and red of the dead, the flies, the maggots. The amnesia of the drunken father who lashes out and then subsides. Does not remember, so the dark bird is not allowed to remember. She must not remember.

Murder control in the night upon a lonely promontory. Murder control in the stabbing and piercing and the sawing after. Murder control in the impulse, the pulse, of the black grasshoppers chirping and creeping across the sands. Feasting on whatever tiny limped or crawled or scuttled. Needling the dark bird's mind with intel through their shells.

An arm she did not remember ripping from a body. Murder control. Until the light and the subsiding in the dark bird of the impulse. Amnesia. Maniac. Dragging the broken wing in the stutter-start dance of the victim. Practice for the next time. Oracle of a future visited upon others. Dragging it as penance through the sweltering day. Under the stunning absence of judgment that was the eternal sky.

The buzz-buzz-listing motion of the Company's commands, counterweight to the broken wing, arrived less and less. That sudden creep become a lunge breaching the dark bird's skull. Some soft creature become armored once inside her brain. Trapped by bone, vocal to get out, to manifest in a wing that twists into blade. Swift sharp beak, the demons of twinned talons.

7 7 7 7 7 7 7 7

3 3 3

10, 0

"We shall fight the 3, we shall live within the 7."

"We shall be the Company in both the 0 and the 10."

The battered journal with the numbers and so many words lay inside the dark bird's nest, wherever it rested for the night. Nests hidden all over the City, and the comfort in that. But rest, not sleep. The dark bird never slept. The

monster that lived inside the dark bird would never sleep. Would not let her sleep, and that stirred up rage.

Words that sounded like numbers, too. Coordinates launched at her, lodged in the flesh of another life, hidden inside her. Gave away its position, became her position. They spewed like soft pebbles or maggots, spilled out onto the sand. By that time they had turned liquid, spat, coagulating in the sun. Nothing but blood. No pattern to discern. No pattern to discern. No task to impart but blood.

10, 7, 3, 0.

If the dark bird lingered too long on the numbers, strayed from the relentless patrol, the preset directives, the monster rose from within and the broken wing turned and turned ever-more frantic.

To detect intruders. To be vigilant. To thwart the three whenever they might appear, encoded and included, a legion of want divined from need. For the Company building needed little now except to rest, to automate, to set boundaries, a sun perpetually setting. A shining scimitar. A beak dipped in gore.

Murder control.

Keeping the journal safe, but not knowing why, because no one knew why. Able to read from it without opening it. Because even a dark bird could be bored, waiting for the next murder control. Because the commands leaking out invisible from the Company came fewer and fewer, and the presets ground down in time, some of them nubs of suggestions for violence, so if she chose violence, she chose it. The dark bird chose it.

Out across the night, a leviathan was dying near the

holding ponds, killed by a flying monster. Out across the night, something emerged from the carcass in its last moments that the dark bird thought she recognized. A person. One of the three, yet not one of the three. But she had no edict from the Company to intervene, and knew this meant the flying monster had taken over her role. Which made the thing inside her furious.

Murder control, read me a story. Murder control, read me a story so I can sleep. Or so the thing inside me can.

Any story at all will do.

~ The Magical Garden ~

I have a magic garden in a secret room. I have the voice of God in my head. I have the voice of my father in my head, too. But I have a magic garden in a secret room. It is there that I hide this journal for now, but not for later. There that I fix the mistakes. I pile the mistakes in the corner of the magic garden with so many beautiful animals and plants. My duck is there. I remember when she was a duckling. When she would be frightened when I entered the magic garden, although I had left her at the top, at the very top, where she could thrive. There was so much to eat, among my mistakes. It was a land of plenty and it was my secret.

When my father brought me to the Company for good and all, I did not at first hear from God or the Company. I heard only from my father, and he put me in charge of extinguishing the broken things, the discards. I did this faithful for several years as his apprentice. I would extinguish the broken things. I would put them in the wood chopper or I

would drown them or I would poison them. Each to its own passing. Whatever seemed to make sense, and not because I wanted to. No, I wanted to fix them. But I wasn't allowed to, because the Company didn't want them fixed and so my father didn't want them fixed either.

Do you understand? Nothing thrives without being broken. Nothing exists without being dead first. I could not escape the voice of God, the voice of the Company. It would boom through like God. Like the Company. And who could say which was better or best? I could not. If it was not God, then it was the Company, and if it was not the Company, then it must be the ghost of my father, curled up inside of my brain, my mind, my skull. I could not get it out if I drilled a hundred holes in there all at once. I could only get it out if I did what the voice said.

The voice of God. The voice of the Company. Which both came later, but came loud like blaring horns and after my father had put me to sleep for some time, and when I woke I ran my hand across rough sutures on the back of my skull. The voice rang true enough, then. It could not be escaped, any more than I could escape my father, and yet, still, there was no *person* other than my father to respond to.

And the voice of the Company, IT said, EXPAND AND MULTIPLY. And IT said, FIX YOUR MISTAKES. (But that is what my father said, too, but my father was not the Company.)

And the voice of the Company, IT said, TAKE THE OTHER AND REMAKE IT AS YOURSELF.

And the voice of the Company, IT said, IF YOU FAIL, WE WILL REMAKE YOU.

But this I giggled at through my tears, for my father

remade me every day. He slapped me and kicked me and shouted when I made mistakes, and I made so many mistakes because I didn't know how to do anything. And he would stave in my skull and I would wake up on the slab. And he would drive a kitchen knife into my heart and I would wake up on the slab. And he would break my legs with a steel pipe and then break my neck and I would wake up on the slab. All of this away from the others, to whom he would talk in a calm voice while consulting ancient tomes and, perhaps, taking off his glasses that he might bite upon the edge of them, in deep thought.

"We'll fix you, we'll fix you. Mind not the pain, son, it's the price of the fixing. Everything dead can be brought back to life, so who minds a little pain, son." As he suffocated me with a plastic bag because the creature had three legs, not four.

I cannot pretend this was not agony, but agony repeated so many times is a different kind of suffering.

"I made you so I'll fix you," he said, matter-of-fact, but I knew my mother had made me too, and if we were dead and merciful, it was not because this was false. But because it was true, and my father could not bear the sharing of the credit. For the mistake that he would fix.

So my father removed any memory of my mother from me—from every part of me. I could not tell you now the color of her eyes or what she wore or what her voice sounded like or what she smelled like. Did she hug me or keep me at arm's length? Did she feed me breakfast, or toss a pail full of parts in my direction across a dirty floor? There is none of that left.

So my father fixed me and kept fixing me and at some point I was fixed enough for him, perhaps because I had grown larger, perhaps because he was bored. And I did not have to die every day but was put to work making things die. And because I knew what it was to die, and because I knew how it was to come back, I tried to make it pleasant, to make it count. Things should be fixed and pinned and certain, like the numbers the Company found so important, the 10 and the 0, the 3 and the 7. They should not be the opposite of that. Thus, my father, I realized later, was so frightened of the Company that he fixed me out of fear that he was not doing right by the Company and had no control over that distant entity or even the numbers but only over me.

Or it could be that he liked to hurt me and there was no one to stop him.

Listen:

Once there was a boy-man who had a magical garden. He hid it behind the laboratory, at first nothing more than a large storage closet that no one else used, that was where his father made him sleep after his mother died. The boy-man who we will call Charlie, and leave off the X for now, took all of his mistakes that he could hide there. In part, to avoid the dying all over again. In part, because Charlie did believe he could save them. Just not in the laboratory, not at the wall of globes, and not at the holding ponds (which did not fix anything but simply let the unfixed escape to pollute the world).

Charlie remade his mistakes into good things and found

his bones less cracked the more he restored in the magical garden and the less he tried to fix in the laboratory. Everyone was happy in that place. Charlie made them happy, and even, perhaps, taught some of them to smile who would not, ordinarily, be wont to smile. Charlie was glad when they weren't sad, because if they were sad, he would have to make them glad.

There grew in that sacred space a tiny empire of wonders, of creatures spliced together, each to save the other, and things that hobbled but still yearned for life not snuffed. There were plants that formed miniature cathedrals for the row of faces Charlie could not reattach to torsos and benches of tough vegetal life glowing red, green, purple upon which lay the torsos Charlie kept alive with their brains embedded within them. There grew up in this weed-filled garden of all that was possible, birds stuck to the end of leaves and flapping wings in midair. There thrived lizards emerging snake-tongue-like from the midst of poppy blooms, an eviscerated green to the arterial red of the flowers.

Always sad, always philosophical, that the good of the whole must outweigh the individual, as the Company voice decreed.

How else to explain, except that in the magical garden, the son recognized that "to fix" meant "to make into a better self." Why fix the thing in place, in its former place, like a butterfly on a killing board? Pretty, but there was always something better it could be, under the son's watchful guidance.

Every night before bedtime, the son would have a wonderful playtime with these creatures of their own creation.

In that green and verdant closet, with so many miniatures of what the son hoped would someday be life-size. Charlie would lie down behind the false wall among the velveteen crush of so many hands and hooves and claws and webbed feet, the rough and the smooth and the lacerated, and surrender to that embrace, find a kind of peace. To let the voices of the fixed lull him to half sleep. To be enraptured in that space and that living bed. Certain that someday soon the magical garden might lawfully spill out into the wider world and his father would understand and the Company would understand, and so, too, might God.

But instead, one night too soon Charlie found his father at the door to the room, one hand on the doorknob, and Charlie could not look upon his father's face, for the glow of satisfaction, the wide, wide grin was too much to bear, and by this look bestowed upon him knew he would be fixed again.

Except the fixing took yet another form this time.

For his father threw open the door to the magical garden and said, "I have prepared a feast for you, for all of your hard, hard work, my son. And I have used only the finest ingredients. Your own ingredients."

There, upon a long table, lay dead and cooked all those creatures I had kept hidden for so long. Every single one, silent and flame-besotted, save the duck, which he knew I loved and he must have loved, too, in his way.

"And you must eat it all," my father whispered in my ear. "You and the bird both. Every last scrap, between you."

And thus the bird and I set to our feast with vigor, even as the tears trickled down my face and I felt as weak and exposed as anything my father had worked on splayed across

the cutting boards in his laboratory. My nerves a network like a brittle starfish and my father breaking off pieces with no regard for the pattern.

Ah, Mother, even if I knew your face, how could this not be hell?

Another time, for time was fluid to the dark bird and she could not always distinguish between them, or moments stacked atop one another so there was no difference, no difference at all.

Night had dropped against sky once again, a kidnapping that held the dark bird close, and sometimes the bird sagged inside that darkness as if trapped in some rough black cloth that stank of surgery. It worried at the dark bird, worried at her like the stars were the tips of thorns and it had become stuck in a thicket of them.

Out in the City, members of some cult, going door to door in a broken shantytown neighborhood, hadn't noticed the duck in the shadow out of the sun. Some broken cult that couldn't contain itself, must be known by all, all must be in it, even though there were so few. The dark bird had slaughtered them when it meant to ignore, something in their demeanor bringing out the rage. Murder control bereft, the monster still in its home in her skull. So she had killed them all on her own. A seepage that startled. Nothing beatific in the remains, fly-studded but quiet.

There came again light under the blackened sky, there

on the lonely hill where she had a nest—become starful against recollection, and grand and rich and also drenched in gray or light purple or even the moon. Soaked by the moon, the blackness, so it felt like cold river water, a comfort upon the dark bird's face and beak.

There came no call from a Company outpost. No admonition to attack, to defend. No alert. Just the night, and some sense of the foxes out on the desert floor, the ones she despised, feared, envied. No one bound them. No voice owned them out of blue sky or velvet night.

But she waited in that place. For the tiny creatures to come out, the ones that could not know her type or her purpose or her past. If the dark bird remained still and silent, she could live in that moment, watching. Unspoiled by any impulse to snatch them up in her beak, to crunch, gnaw, or devour.

The nighttime blossoms registered black to human sight, but to her a glittering field of yellow and blue and saffron—pinprick flowers in multitudes—arose on slender stalks, and with them the smell of lavender and rosemary and mint. Smells, almost, from another world, deployed by the flowers as a kind of trap, a memory of things that no longer existed. For they were clever flowers, almost worthy of the magical garden.

Came with the flowers, weaving through them, a scrabbling of some mutant desert rat, then the tingle-hops of the three long legs, and a grappling as of two of them at play, sproing and spring, then gone. Came a fast-sharp slither of a two-tailed snake, headed after to eat the insects dislodged by their passage. Then peering out, subsonic arguments

tin-tin-tin in the dark bird's ears, alcohol minnows, whose gills distilled moisture from sand, stitching in and out, the glint the glint the glint. Their small dramas played out before this statue of a dark bird.

The way the mice chased the grasshoppers and the grasshoppers pretended to be flower stalks . . .

Idyllic, could have been to be silent nocturnal, on a hill, on a darkling plain. To not think. To not conflict with the internal. To watch the stars. But:

Murder control. Murder control. Feasting of a sudden on good gristle meat. Delicate ankle. Elbow. Feasting in the dank dim glow. Unpredictable. Let loose. Loosened. The rage so familiar, like breathing, that the dark bird felt only the aftermath, which was a kind of weakening.

Why should this impulse always be impulsive. Unable to tell if there had been a command, because there was now just an echo. Was it the echo of a command? Or was it nothing?

Comforting weight of the journal beneath the dark bird.

Murder control, read me another story. Just one more story. One about me, this time.

No matter how terrible?

No matter how terrible.

Even if it's not really about you?

I know all the stories are really about him.

~ The Ugly Duckling ~

My father always said, "I'll whip you if you don't get it right," so let us pretend I got it right in the end because it was never as gentle as whipping. But not every being can get it

right the first time. I do not blame some in the magical garden. Their heads were not on right or not right away. Their angles were all wrong. They could never be like my duck. My duck was my luck, my pluck. I could never call it dark bird like the others.

But she was a duck—a plucky duckling who existed atop a hedgerow pedestal made of flesh in the magical garden. Queen of that place. Queen of my childhood. Duckling eternal. For I'd had the dark bird as a duckling for twenty years before she became a duck. A foundling found when I was but a child of seven. Or ten. Or zero. Or three. One of those. And she was left on our doorstep.

But where was that doorstep? Erased with my mother is every place I ever lived before the Company building. Should she be a hologram or holograsp beyond reach, I ask only that she once was real, so that I am too. What became confused is whether the provenance of flesh should sit heavy on the mind shoved inside.

My father always said, "Make this into a lesson or I'll kill it. And you. Again."

The Company, IT always said, BE EFFICIENT, BE INGENIOUS.

The Company, IT always said, IF IT DIES, IT WAS MEANT TO DIE.

The Company, IT always said, MAKE THIS INTO A LESSON OR I'LL KILL IT. AND YOU. AGAIN.

So I did. I made the duckling my first project: to arrest the aging process so the duckling would be forever young. Fluffy and fuzzy and never quack but instead make querulous ducking noises. Sometimes I gave the duckling

three wings, sometimes one wing. Sometimes wings atop its head.

But always it had feathers and a head and a torso, though over time I found ways to splice the lizardacious onto her in ways that made her fuzzling beauty ever-more glowing and gorgeous, and locked her duckling self in place. Almost by mistake.

I had no mother but that duckling, or I was a mother to the duckling that became a duck. I was never a mother or a father but a friend to the duckling, and to all in the magical garden.

Listen:

Listen, yet how shall I mean it, because who is reading but me? Who will ever read this but me and in the ramble I can lose my thoughts lose my mind, forget even more until someday it will all be in here, or it will be lost forever. That much I learned from Sarah.

Once upon a time there was a torture garden, I mean a magical garden, that was destroyed by an evil sorcerer who happened to be a father who should never have had a child.

Everyone who lived within the magical garden, other than the duckling, was cooked and served at a vast banquet of the sweet and the savory and devoured whole or in slices or casseroles. It was terrible and beautiful and it was going

to happen whether the son ate of his creations or not. What could they know of the bite and crunch by then?

God and the Company, IT decreed, DEVOUR and the devouring began and never ended.

After the banquet, the boy wizard, Charlie, fell into disrepair and despair. Even after the success of the blue fox (who could not be found) for the Company. Even as the Company spread so far and wide it became a vast mouth swallowing everything. Nothing in the boy wizard's studies or experiments could lift his spirits. There were only the Company edicts, come from farther and farther away as their version of the City drifted from the center. The portal wall grew hazy and the vision of the original City on the banks of a vibrant river so distant. And the boy wizard could care less.

God not but Company yes, IT commanded, ALCHEMIZE THE FLESH TO BECOME THE WALLS. ADD TO THE WALL OF GLOBES EACH NEW ONE OF THE 7.

God or the Company, IT ordered, PRODUCE THE OTHERS THAT MIGHT POPULATE THE 7 AND FIGHT THE 3. YOU HAVE TEN SECONDS. 10, 9, 8, 7, 6, 5 . . .

Or this is just something I thought of now.

Charlie, through his gloom, wrestling with the proteins and the vocal cords and the sinew and the blood and the epidermis, to within those 10 create more magic, even with the magical garden dead. For the 7. Against the 3. Although he did not then really grasp who the 3 were, or how they might collude with the fox. The fox was the 1 or the 0. He became confused, like in all fairy tales retold and updated so

what had been certain and sacrosanct sank into disavowal, disavowel, disembowelment.

How do you know you're in hell, if God and Company are still conversing with you? Or is that how you know?

This continued for years.

My father transformed my face into that of a bat. My father slit my throat and inserted surgical mice. My father rearranged my organs so they spelled out the true name of the Company inside. 10, 7, 3, 0.

But chance or fortune or fate favorited Charlie in the end. For there came a day at the vats when his father fell, temporary consumed by fumes or poison or to the lacerating regard of a self-made creature whose dagger-quality to the eyes was in fact a propulsive sliver, lodging in my father's neurological epicenters. It is still hard to tell why he fell even so, why he toppled like a cut tree, there in the laboratory. It seemed impossible. This toppling. Like the cutting of a tree in the yard of the house of my youth that no one, not even I, can remember. The tree you could not fit your arms around when you hugged it, the tree was so huge. Such a monster could never fall.

Nor did I understand why all looked to the boy-king Charlie to heal him.

And so the father died and the son cried while inside his mind he laughed so hard he cried. He laughed and laughed so hard his organs regained their natural places and blood seeped from his ears and his nose. But that was just because he was so unnatural now.

As my first act—I mean the son's act—taking his place, the son forbade his removal from the vats, to preserve him,

that some part of him might live on in the creatures I would create, and the ones I would save. For it was then that I set up the magical garden again, in plain view. And in this new magical garden there were many pools of healthy water and some that were muddy and stands of tall grasses and an artificial sun. But mostly there I hid and saved the parts and bits that mewled and would have been snuffed, and upon that pile, that throne, sat my duckling.

And perhaps duckling she would always have remained, to remind me of my smiling youth and my father and all of the other good, good things that had come my way.

But that, too, is when the voice of the Company came into my head, or perhaps it was the ghost of the ghost of my mother. In the last days, who could tell the difference? That was when the Company told me to transform the duckling into a duck. A duck with a broken wing. And to house what remained of my father's brain within the duck.

And I believe it was a test for all of my days—that the Company wanted me to sacrifice the thing I had the most pride in, that I might no longer have pride and that I might obey the Company in all things.

So I made my duckling into a duck, and I did this in the blink of an eye. After twenty years, the duckling became the dark bird in only the space and slice of an eye. A day and a night. But it did not drive her mad. It made her greater than herself. I swear it. What drove her mad was the mission where she brought back Sarah, and I will not talk about that. It was not my fault.

And when things began to go bad all the way through, I was not to blame. I had been the one to listen to the voice in

my head, even after I wasn't sure if it was still from the Company but instead from God. I was the one who had rescued so many lost souls by remaking them in the magical garden.

But I could not predict Nocturnalia anymore, no how know how, for it had gotten beyond us. But I could not understand how chaos could be controlled all across the City because I did not know how no how it could be controlled within my self.

O and lo, then I needed the dark bird ever more, for so many special missions. To hold back the end of it all. To hold firm. To give me time. Which was all I ever needed, from beginning to end.

The dark bird that was the duckling that was me. That was my father.

Fly away dark bird, fly away. Far from here. With your broken wing.

I am mad, you see, and know it. And yet I know things.

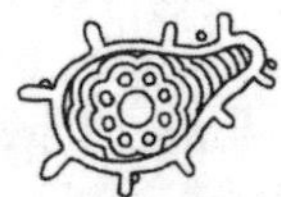

Murder control clicking like a switch flipped like a click like a cut like a blood-covered switch that clicked . . . *off.* For a time.

Nocturnalia. Out upon the darkling plain, the tired dance of the broken wing. Brought to a halt by the thought of fire. The thought of what lay behind and what lay ahead being so the same. Passenger only. Passenger enslaved to fury. Some of it her own fury at being so encaptured and enraptured. Her own true nature. Inescapable, but one day perhaps would escape it.

Out there, one night, between being called forth. Between being the dark bird and just a duck with a mind of its own. Before the next possession. Came the vast slather of night wings above and the aerobatic capture of insects and, sometimes, like a lacy overlay on the dark bird's mind, the invisible sonar of bats, inquiring and then rebuffed. For the dark bird was a dead space, but one that colonized if they lingered too long.

Came, too, in the absolute dead of one night, with no moon and the stars reduced to smudges, a shape-shifter exiled to that place. Exiled like something made and not now used. Manifest as several creatures at once, anchored to a writhing flat black pedestal. Registering as too many coordinates, a creature that had become a map.

"I'll kill you," the duck told the shape-shifter. "I'll kill you and feast on your entrails."

"You are not a duck."

"You are not a whatever you are."

"I'm out of place. I'm not meant to be here. Soon, I won't be."

Surprise at approximation of speech, which the shape-shifter, as a shape-shifter will, supplied . . . and all the rage snuffed out and no directive from the Company. The shape-shifter interfered with the signal. The burst was there, the burst-burst-burst, but sputtering, sputtered.

"Are you something that rhymes with duck?" the shape-shifter asked. "The ghost with the face of a bat used to mutter all the words that rhyme with duck."

"I know nothing of that."

The duck could not tell if the shape-shifter spoke for her,

because the words didn't sound like her words. But, then, she didn't know what her words might sound like in this language.

"There are versions that are not versions at all but only Source. Yet the old man only keeps moving through versions. He's fractured."

"I'm not supposed to see him, but I do. I just pretend not to."

"Bad luck. Bad duck. Sad, sad pluck."

"Why are you out here?" A shape-shifter could be anything in the City, did not need to live as outcast.

"Because so few want me in there. Because it's safer here. Besides, I've learned to like it here. It's quiet. I can be alone."

"I like it, too. I like the quiet. I like the stars."

They looked up at the stars for a time.

"You cannot kill me," the duck said, finally, after what analysis was left to it. "Or absorb me."

"I know. That's why I like you. And you like me."

"Who made you?"

"I don't know. Who made you?"

"I've forgotten. Perhaps the person who lives inside me."

"Like a pit in a plum?"

"Like a pit."

"Maybe the pit can't see the old man. Pit to prune, not receiving."

"I don't know what that means."

"Yes you do." And she did and the shape-shifter asked, "Is the pit where the rage comes from?"

"Do you feel the salamanders falling?"

The creature turned ten eyes up toward the heavens. It was true. The night was a mist of lightly falling amphibians. So tiny, delicate. Each a memory of a time and place where she had almost been free. But not quite.

"It's amazing. It's perfect. Perfecto. Perfection. Purr."

The shape-shifter began to purr like a cat. The dark bird had never seen a real cat, but the shape-shifter put the image of a contented cat in her mind.

"The ground feels better after, beneath my feet. Even though they are gone."

"It's really a person. It was a person. Now it's so many things. I wonder if the person is happy now. So distributed."

"Happy is a human concept."

"I'm not human and I want to be happy."

"Are you happy in this moment?"

"Yes."

"Then that is enough."

For the dark bird, for it was all she had.

"I like the wind, too."

The wind over the desert floor now was a shushing and rushing and a swirl that brought with it the cold cool embrace of fragrant scents from beyond the City. The reassurance that there was a place beyond the City. Out of mind.

"What will you do—after?" the shape-shifter asked.

"After what?" asked the dark bird.

"After the end of it all. After the rains. After all the resolves resolve."

"I don't know. What will you do?"

"Nothing. I won't be here anymore."

"How do you know?"

"I just know. But you will be here. You will live here."

The dark bird, the ugly duckling, frantic: "Can you help me? There is this thing in my head. A poison. A command. A rot. A presence. I cannot get it out. I do terrible things. I do terrible, terrible things."

"So do I."

"So you understand."

"I do."

"Can you help?"

A barrier against the slaughter. The slaughterous impulse that came in exterior and inhabited.

Killing the pale men on the other Earth invaded by the Company. Killing them because she could.

"I am going into your mind now. I am in your mind, in the future. When you are older and weaker. I can see into your mind there, then, not now. I am snapping the connection. I am snapping the cord. So it will be alone, quarantined, the mad thing inside you. It will live there, but cannot access you."

"And now?"

"You must live with it until you catch up to the future. But one day, you can just be a duck again."

"Just."

The shape-shifter laughed. "I am just a squid that lives on land. I am a dog that is a cat. I am a bird that is a lizard. I am mighty, except I am weak." And the shape-shifter chortled and guffawed and made the duck feel jolly and kind and at peace.

I am the ugly duckling that survived the magical garden. I am worth something. I am not just a monster.

"Do you ever wonder?" she asked the shape-shifter. "Do you ever wonder what it would be like not to live in the world of humans?"

The shape-shifter considered that a moment, made a sound like a sad laugh or a weeping chuckle. Shook off the question.

"Shall I tell you a story before I leave?" the shape-shifter asked. "It's a story that should be in the journal, but it isn't. The story isn't about you, but it is about you."

"Yes, you can tell me a story. I would like that."

"Once upon a time, in an age of too many monsters, a blue fox appeared across the drifting sands . . ."

9. CAN'T FORGET

v.3.1

i.

to the murderous child

They killed me. They brought me back. They killed me. They brought me back. They killed me. They brought me back. They killed me. They brought me back. They killed me. They brought me back. They killed me. They brought me back. They killed me. They brought me back. They killed me. They brought me back. They killed me. They brought me back. They killed me. They brought me back. They killed me. They brought me back. They killed me. They brought me back. They killed me. They brought me back. They killed me. They brought me back. They killed me. They brought me back. They killed me. They brought me back. They killed

me. They brought me back. They killed me. They brought me back. They

killed me. They brought me back. They killed me. They brought me back.

They killed me. They brought me back. They killed me. They brought me back.

They killed me. They brought me back. They killed me. They brought me back.

One time I escaped.

You want. Things to be words. That are not words. Could never be words. Your *fox* is some other construct. We did not agree to that. We do not call ourselves *foxes*. A thing you created that is not me. To think an autopsy was a person. To think a dissection meant a type of mind. If I went rummaging through your carcass, would I find you?

But I will give you words. Tell it the way you can hear it. Not natural to me. Every word that spills out of me and reaches you is lost. I lose so much in this moment. Talking to you. Needing to talk to you. But in the end, you will give the words back to me in different form. And that will feel like something ripped from you.

Think of me as a magician, child. Except I show you what is already there. Invisible only to you. That is the trick.

A stale, shabby trick that I must show to you. But that is the stale, shabby trick your senses have played on you. You make your disease into our disease. You make us into a disease because you are sick.

Smell can be a wall or a tunnel or a word scrawled across pine needles soft against a forest floor. It can be tortuous, kind, humble, vainglorious. Even the least hint of it can be a history of betrayal or of friendship. To you, it is simpler. Much too simple.

What use are certain words to you if you cannot inhabit them? Ears and tongues and the places that slink back to report to a fox but never to you. Lines created by waterscent, lines fuzzy and sharp. Heat. Cascading or still. The ever-shifting, ever-sharing smell of other foxes. The noise of a porcupine that becomes a taste on the tongue that lingers. The supersonic laughing of rats. The rich, heady smell of a bear plodding through.

Still, I burrow deeper. Still, you will follow me.

Human is a stronghold that hides a weakness.

Once upon a time, there was a fox who became an astronaut. He did not like it much. It hurt to become an astronaut. It hurt to be so still. Copse. Corpse. Dead cool place under moonlight. I had made a meal of the small, became small myself, plucked and imprisoned by the Company. They wanted to eat me, but not in the usual way.

Cages of dead animals all around, in their sacred place, their laboratory. Dead and sick and wounded and drugged and deranged. Men, too, unmoving, stacked in the corners. There were so many of them pale. Stark. Scentless. Soundless. Soulless. Yet they heard sound, held it. Within. Could see and smell and all the rest. Yet lay in closets and alcoves. Stiff. Unyielding. Less human than a fox.

I was just another animal in a cage to be sacrificed. For a task that might or might not work. For the Company. They had to send the one, if they could. Get the one back. Start over if they couldn't. Easier than building more. Open a way. Close a way. I should have gone insane but I was a fox, not a human. I was only made to last four years. I was used to death, in that way, through the generations.

I was intelligent already. They tried to make me more human. Intelligent in the way humans call themselves intelligent. So I held on deep to fox. They couldn't risk a human, but they wanted a human response. Apes and dogs, rats and cats—all died. But a fox? A fox knows a burrow. A fox digs a hole in the ground, a fox jumps through the hole it created, pulls the hole in after it. Where is the fox now?

They made my brain more distributed. Stave in my skull and still my feet could think, carry me from danger, devise a strategy, chart the coordinates home. Turned me half into equation, one that could adapt to destination.

"All flesh is quantum." One torturer to another, conversing over the half corpse. Who could hear them. Understand them. Could have leapt up and torn out at least one throat before the end.

But I was smarter than that.

As the aliens hovered above me, tinkering with me. Syringed. Rolled over. Shaved. Dipped. Banded. Sent forth.

Was I the first fox? Or just the last? I would never know.

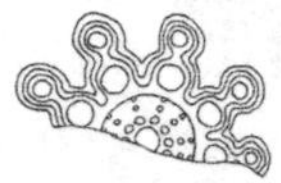

Charlie in the Corner, I called him, once I knew what language was. Son of the head researcher. The one who always watched, recommended never *did*, back then. He was bright and white and shiny and fresh. Not yet monstrous in appearance. He must have thought himself fresh and full of life. To me, already, he was full of death. Burgeoning with maggots.

Charlie the Watcher. Scribbling in his journal. Good for nothing. Except he liked the guts of it. He liked to get in the guts. The autopsies of what went wrong. I noticed him for that.

The fervor. The enthusiasm. There were times I thought Charlie had created this "father," that the father was just the son's puppet, a mask or disguise.

It was from Charlie's worm-mouth that I first heard *Nocturnalia*, but only later understood what he meant.

All the smells of death and decay in that place. I hated that place because it turned the smells foxes love into smells a fox could come to hate.

I came to hate the mechanism of my departure, too. It was small at first. A small biomechanical creature. It mewled and wet the bed and at first I thought as it grew beside me, us connected by tubes, that it was my friend. Or a comrade

in our distress. But it was the door being grown to attune to me, for this experiment. Strange dreams from that amniotic fluid. Strange dreams of the universe, of burrows with no end. With chambers as large as a world and stars trickling down the sides of stone. The wealth of smells the universe hid, that the door gave to me all unknowing! As I shared its dreams, translated into fox.

One day it would devour me and I would be someplace else.

There was left just the inconvenience of needles and grubs—all the biotech put in the fox that it learns to subvert and to hack. Because my torturers didn't understand the fox mind, the fox body.

They gave me telescopic sight and made me hate them more that my world was no longer the richness of smell and taste and hearing, and now I must adjust to this cacophony of images, un-fox-like.

Or: I once saw a frog paralyzed by a spider and cocooned in its webbing. Numb and spiraling and slowly being eaten. Now I was the frog, but the cocoon was alive and devouring me. Then I became the cocoon.

You wouldn't understand me even if I made sense. Before the wall of globes. There was just one globe against a vast wall and it wanted to eat me and I was in the globe and I was everywhere and I was nowhere, too. I was the one sent. Every time. It was on this side. It was alive. Sent

out across time, space. Trying to destroy my mind. As side effect.

I plotted revenge. I cursed them silently: Let them be sent on journeys no one ever had. Let them be strapped to the gurney, needled and cut and scanned. Let them be filled with the sluggish liquid from syringes. Let them be filled with worms and beetles and dead leaves or the feeling of dead leaves crinkling and cracking to dust inside. Let them go forth as the experiment, curled up inside a globe, a globe, a globe pushed out across the face of the deep. Of many depths. Let them know the emptiness.

The battlefield that was my body.

Let them know the way it hurt somewhere so basic, so plain, so laid bare, that I could not hide from it. I could not hide could not fight could not kill myself but was only ever forced to leap and lunge into the effort. Forced to return. But I was always dead when I came back. They couldn't fix that, consequences of coordinates, of fixing coordinates, of the struggle to know what *mind* meant, what they meant by *body* or even *journey*. To form a map, to advance the borders of the map, even as the compass was no use.

They had changed my genes. I could breathe without air. I could breathe without body or mind. In water. Buried deep in the earth. They opened my head, fixed me like switchblades flickering and snickering, my thoughts thick as smoke and swirling, cut and recut, toward the ceiling. Only so I could go back again. Go black again.

My mind had had enough. My mind gave everything up. I gave it all up in the moment. I wanted nothing of me left, nothing they could put back together. Would've smashed it

with a rock until you couldn't recognize it. But that was just my mind. My body didn't agree. My body wanted to fight back. My body wanted to murder them all until the walls were covered in blood and the floor and it smashed down the door to that place. My body knew what my mind did not.

Would there ever be a way out?

Dread coordinates. A compass in my head that spun wild. Picked up the scent. Found the trail. Disintegrated into molecules.

Fragments are what I have.

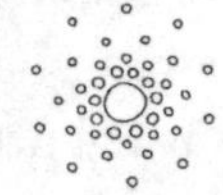

the coded sky and the scaffolding
brought to the other place through the eye
there came the blurring speed, the blurring of speed
and the stillness in the midst of motion
there was the burning speed and the stillness
the stillness and the burning speed
putting me to the torch putting me to
putting me where i did not
want to be

My house was full of holes already, so they sent me down another. All the burrows of the dark, of the night sky. The stars changed above me, but I was constant beneath them.

I was astronaut and spaceship both. I had no suit. Just my fur. I had no instruments. Just my brain. Devoured, I vaulted space and time. Devoured, I became other other. Another.

What would be the story I made up to understand. I hadn't the luxury. I had to know what it actually was. I had to know. And slowly . . . I did.

Maw tunnel burrow maw.

The first time. Wondrous terrible devouring but still alive. The four panels of mouth unspooling in breach and sough. All encompassing. Breathy and close. The wind rising with the glint of stars within. Oh that close, close friend, chained to me those many months. Untethered only a day, and now the Company fed me to the maw and kept feeding me. Told me to think of it as burrow, but no burrow plunged toward you. No burrow lay thick around and breathed. No burrow made of you in your bubble of air a morsel.

Implosion. Launched. Acceleration and pressure. Until nothing lay around me but darkness and fragments of time that slithered and knocked against me and with the rumble or growl the fresh green beatific scent of corpse. Was I dying to live? Was I released elsewhere as haunt or curling question where once had been flesh? I could hear as up above in the dark of throat a glimmer of deep sound, of sound that held me distant, that cocooned in sonorous discharge the friction of the travel. The hum of engines of flesh. The function of a creature that lived to transport.

O in the middle. Weightless. Thoughtless without guile. Without body. Without mind. The stars not wrapped around me, but something else. Something elemental. The worlds

seen through scrim and skin. No space between me and . . . everything.

It was over in seconds or days or centuries. I was a fiery tail chasing a mind. I was a mind tumbling end over end until the halt.

Vertigo and bewildering color, too sharp for a fox's eyes, and I came to rest on the verge of a vast plateau of wildflowers, their scent the pinprick of itch in some places and the solace of velvet in others. Over the edge to which I'd tumbled and dug in my back paws: a desolation of black ravines and riven places stuck through with machines like mausoleums.

Behind me: nothing. No old friend to devour me back to where I had been. No hint of what had delivered me here.

The shattered splinters of my bones reconstituted. The matter behind my skull bone floated, spun, reconstituted. My legs were my own again. My mind, some semblance.

Then, sudden, from eclipse: the sun. Earth, stung pleasant with the sweet of earthworm and opulent beetle. I dearly wished the joy of triangulation, the pounce based on a good ear's geometry.

But what was I to do here, before hauled back, unwilling servant? Just be: here. All the dead told me that. All the other animals that had failed to survive this journey. Returned in seconds, rancid flayed broken smudges shoveled off to the side. Burned. Bagged. Fed back to other animals that wanted nothing of that meal.

My eyes were the Company's eyes. I was their creature. I'd be caged again. I'd be chained. But I was a fox, nothing human, even now, and so I ran across that meadow like a blue flame. I ran and ran like something free and some-

thing natural and something that knew his destination. I hunted there in that strange place as if the past had never happened, could not touch me.

Until the next time. Until a hundred next times. Oh, I could not say there was no sting, no hind-thought, no scratch of leg on ear. But the grass felt so good. The grass felt so good.

By mistake, they'd gotten it right enough the first time.

Not the second. Not the third. Not the fourth.

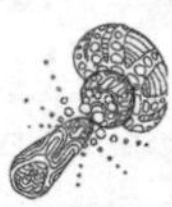

A room is no longer there. Does it still exist?

All the false, wrong coordinates I would occupy. Occupying spaces I wasn't meant to occupy. As they perfected the process. Screaming into the dirt. Screaming into space. Pulled under and through. Dissected. Disembodied. Sent out again.

They even made me like it, sometimes. They made me think of burrows. Of the underground. Of being an explorer. My first human thought. They petted me. They fussed over me. They made me feel brave. And when they tried to pry out my mind, instead they opened up theirs to me. Tunnels. Burrows. I dug my way into them and out into the light.

So I died and then they solved me again, as *fox*, and I lived again in time to be sent back, to another part of the map. As if I were compass and creature both. There came a

whine in the tissue, in the sinews. I feel it still. From the stress of it. If I had not gotten free. If I had not stepped free of it. I might be dying still. Resurrected still.

I couldn't stop them from extracting the intel like sapphires hidden behind my eyes. In my brain. Extracting them with pliers. I was the intent. Shining darkly on their sensors. Reporting back. Through my skin. Though I didn't want to. Inhabited by the relics of worms and leeches and other things that lived inside of me. For a time.

But I grew strong in my invisible globe. They sought to un-fox me, but I out-foxed them. And in the end, they seeded their realities with me. By mistake. Too many microbes and parasites and symbiotes in their broth. Unintended ecosystems that spoke to me.

I remember Charlie, when I returned desiccated, husked, and they put me back together, gathered coordinates and data from me. Charlie did not in those days have an X by his name or over his eyes, sported not a bat head but instead a kind of smooth soft whiteness that wobbled like an imperfect satellite in decaying orbit.

"Was it beautiful?"

"You would not understand." But I did not yet have the curse of human speech, so he heard only yapping.

"But was it beautiful?"

"Someday, Charlie, I'll kill you, and that—that will be beautiful."

But I never did kill him, and in time I almost forgot him, even though now he haunts me every night. Haunts me every day. Child, I can look down from this haunted spot and see him, but he's forgotten me.

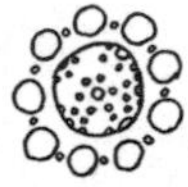

There were times I despaired. On missions to such faraway places. Entered such dark places fated to explore only death, where my thoughts wandered from me as if separate from my mind. Dark eyes staring from the corner of dank burrows. The glint of the eye, that was my trauma, barking back at me.

A terrible joy. A joy in sadness and in pain. A joy, even, in contemplating death.

In time, my fur turned blue. Unintended side effect? A color caught from the lab or from the journey? Anointed by something *out there*, in transit?

Nothing I say with words can be enough.

In time, the Company found what it needed, colonized, spread like contagion.

In time, too, I escaped, yes.

But I wasn't free.

ii.

to the dead people

They killed us with traps. They killed us with poisons. They killed us with snares. They killed us with guns. They killed us with knives. They strangled us. They trampled us. They tore us apart with hounds. They baited steel-jawed traps. They starved us out. They burned us alive. They withheld water. They killed all our prey. They slit our throats. They filled in our burrows. They drowned us. They trampled us under horses' hooves. They bred us for fur and bludgeoned us to death. They kept us in cages so small with so many we burst apart. They suffocated us with poison gas. They strangled us. They put us in sacks and beat us with clubs. They cut out our tongues so we bled to death. They skinned us alive. They detonated rock and stopped our

hearts all unknowing. They swung us by our tails and smashed our skulls against stones. They murdered us in each and every year. They murdered us on each and every day. They killed us with traps. They killed us with poisons. They killed us with snares. They killed us with guns. They killed us with knives. They strangled us. They trampled us. They tore us apart with hounds. They baited steel-jawed traps. They starved us out. They burned us alive. They withheld water. They killed all our prey. They slit our throats. They filled in our burrows. They drowned us. They trampled us under horses' hooves. They bred us for fur and bludgeoned us to death. They kept us in cages so small with so many we burst apart. They suffocated us with poison gas. They strangled us. They put us in sacks and beat us with clubs. They cut out our tongues so we bled to death. They skinned us alive. They detonated rock and stopped our hearts all unknowing. They swung us by our tails and smashed our skulls against stones. They murdered us in each and every year. They murdered us on each and every day. They killed us with traps. They killed us with poisons. They killed us with snares. They killed us with guns. They killed us with knives. They strangled us. They trampled us. They tore us apart with hounds. They baited steel-jawed traps. They starved us out. They burned us alive. They withheld water. They killed all our prey. They slit our throats. They filled in our burrows. They drowned us. They trampled us under horses' hooves. They bred us for fur and bludgeoned us to death. They kept us in cages so small with so many we burst apart. They suffocated us with poison gas. They strangled us. They put us in sacks and beat us with clubs. They cut out our

tongues so we bled to death. They skinned us alive. They detonated rock and stopped our hearts all unknowing. They swung us by our tails and smashed our skulls against stones. They murdered us in each and every year. They murdered us on each and every day. They killed us with traps. They killed us with poisons. They killed us with snares. They killed us with guns. They killed us with knives. They strangled us. They trampled us. They tore us apart with hounds. They baited steel-jawed traps. They starved us out. They burned us alive. They withheld water. They killed all our prey. They slit our throats. They filled in our burrows. They drowned us. They trampled us under horses' hooves. They bred us for fur and bludgeoned us to death. They kept us in cages so small with so many we burst apart. They suffocated us with poison gas. They strangled us. They put us in sacks and beat us with clubs. They cut out our tongues so we bled to death. They skinned us alive. They detonated rock and stopped our hearts all unknowing. They swung us by our tails and smashed our skulls against stones. They murdered us in each and every year. They murdered us on each and every day. They killed us with traps. They killed us with poisons. They killed us with snares. They killed us with guns. They killed us with knives. They strangled us. They trampled us. They tore us apart with hounds. They baited steel-jawed traps. They starved us out. They burned us alive. They withheld water. They killed all our prey. They slit our throats. They filled in our burrows. They drowned us. They trampled us under horses' hooves. They bred us for fur and bludgeoned us to death. They kept us in cages so small with so many we burst apart. They suffocated us with poison gas. They stran-

gled us. They put us in sacks and beat us with clubs. They cut out our tongues so we bled to death. They skinned us alive. They detonated rock and stopped our hearts all unknowing. They swung us by our tails and smashed our skulls against stones. They murdered us in each and every year. They murdered us on each and every day. They killed us with traps. They killed us with poisons. They killed us with snares. They killed us with guns. They killed us with knives. They strangled us. They trampled us. They tore us apart with hounds. They baited steel-jawed traps. They starved us out. They burned us alive. They withheld water. They killed all our prey. They slit our throats. They filled in our burrows. They drowned us. They trampled us under horses' hooves. They bred us for fur and bludgeoned us to death. They kept us in cages so small with so many we burst apart. They suffocated us with poison gas. They strangled us. They put us in sacks and beat us with clubs. They cut out our tongues so we bled to death. They skinned us alive. They detonated rock and stopped our hearts all unknowing. (Everywhere we walk, the desert gives way to the ghosts of trees, of streams.) They swung us by our tails and smashed our skulls against stones. They murdered us in each and every year. They murdered us on each and every day. They killed us with traps. They killed us with poisons. They killed us with snares. They killed us with guns. They killed us with knives. They strangled us. They trampled us. They tore us apart with hounds. (We walk forests like you walk a room you built.) They baited steel-jawed traps. They starved us out. They burned us alive. They withheld water. They killed all our prey. They slit our throats. They filled in our burrows. They drowned us. They

trampled us under horses' hooves. They bred us for fur and bludgeoned us to death. They kept us in cages so small with so many we burst apart. They suffocated us with poison gas. They strangled us. They put us in sacks and beat us with clubs. They cut out our tongues so we bled to death. They skinned us alive. They detonated rock and stopped our hearts all unknowing. They swung us by our tails and smashed our skulls against stones. They murdered us in each and every year. They murdered us on each and every day. They killed us with traps. They killed us with poisons. They killed us with snares. They killed us with guns. They killed us with knives. They strangled us. They trampled us. They tore us apart with hounds. They baited steel-jawed traps. They starved us out. They burned us alive. (But what is too much to bear?) They withheld water. They killed all our prey. They slit our throats. They filled in our burrows. They drowned us. (Not being alive.) They trampled us under horses' hooves. They bred us for fur and bludgeoned us to death. They kept us in cages so small with so many we burst apart. They suffocated us with poison gas. They strangled us. They put us in sacks and beat us with clubs. They cut out our tongues so we bled to death. They skinned us alive. (So we kept being alive even as they destroyed us.) They detonated rock and stopped our hearts all unknowing. They swung us by our tails and smashed our skulls against stones. They murdered us in each and every year. (So we buried our secrets though they tried to extinguish our secrets with us.) They murdered us on each and every day. They killed us with traps. They killed us with poisons. They killed us with snares. They killed us with guns. They killed us with knives.

They strangled us. They trampled us. They tore us apart with hounds. They baited steel-jawed traps. They starved us out. They burned us alive. They withheld water. They killed all our prey. They slit our throats. They filled in our burrows. They drowned us. They trampled us under horses' hooves. They bred us for fur and bludgeoned us to death. They kept us in cages so small with so many we burst apart. They suffocated us with poison gas. They strangled us. They put us in sacks and beat us with clubs. They cut out our tongues so we bled to death. They skinned us alive. They detonated rock and stopped our hearts all unknowing. (Up until this very day.) They swung us by our tails and smashed our skulls against stones. They murdered us in each and every year. They murdered us on each and every day. They killed us with traps. They killed us with poisons. They killed us with snares. They killed us with guns. They killed us with knives. They strangled us. They trampled us. They tore us apart with hounds. They baited steel-jawed traps. They starved us out. They burned us alive. They withheld water. They killed all our prey. They slit our throats. They filled in our burrows. They drowned us. They trampled us under horses' hooves. They bred us for fur and bludgeoned us to death. They kept us in cages so small with so many we burst apart. They suffocated us with poison gas. They strangled us. They put us in sacks and beat us with clubs. They cut out our tongues so we bled to death. They skinned us alive. They detonated rock and stopped our hearts all unknowing. (They keep coming; they never stop.) They swung us by our tails and smashed our skulls against stones.

You couldn't kill us all.

What is too much to bear? Not being alive is too much to bear. We kept being alive even as they destroyed us. We kept our secrets though they tried to extinguish our secrets with us. Still we died. Still we lived. Up until this day.

A fox must set itself on fire to become human, the old myths say. But they never say whether if you set a human on fire they become a fox. Perhaps because no human could live up to being a fox. You are a common species. Or were a common species. A common. In the commons. A common domain.

After I escaped, I lived in a cabin up in the woods for a time. Which woods when is unimportant.

Let me tell you a story about a story I read in the cabin. In the story, there was a parrot imprisoned for sixty years. At the end of the story, the parrot forgave his captor because his captor was an astronomer and looked noble at the stars.

After I read that story, I started killing humans.

Made a sport of trapping humans. I trapped them, I snared them, I poisoned them. I shot them. I cut them. I used arrows on them. I drowned humans. I crushed them. I drove over them. All around in clearings you'd see dead humans. No one took any mind. All the mind was gone, in the place I'd chosen.

It was like a nightmare. It was like a dream. But I was a fox. How could I do any of that? Maybe it *was* a dream or a nightmare. Maybe it was *just* a story.

What do you think, human? Do you think I could do that?

A vast golden hotel shaped like a ship had fallen on its side into a ravine and could not right itself. All of the people had sloshed out of the pool at the top of the ark, fallen to their deaths. Their bodies lay rotting and dull red. Ripped apart, vessels filling up with mold and standing water. Faces frozen in less a scream than a monumental disbelief that their monument had failed them.

The rest we killed.

Except the chef, who raged at me that he had so much work to do that day. That he must be allowed to prepare the kitchen. The rows of kitchens. The rows of larders full of stinking maggoty meat. For all of the dead guests. What was wasted was no less or no more than what was wasted before the fall.

The concierge cowered next to him, begging forgiveness for the words of the chef.

But the words meant nothing to me. *Kitchen* meant nothing to me. All the sunken, skewed tables and beds and chairs and sofas and slanted paintings, stinking of the poisons they released. All the useless chandeliers broken across the pointless marbled floors. Nothing. What a nothing you made out of the world you were given.

I let them go. Watched them running across the devastated landscape. Where were they going? The whole world was like this.

The cook and his concierge, the concierge and his cook. Dancing into oblivion. And as they receded into the landscape, the words *cook* and *concierge* fled with them, became tiny. Were no more.

With all the murder and the killing and the chaos of warfare, there was little time to talk to my prey. But I talked to some.

There was the artist who believed we were all sacred as he begged me for a ham hock or any scrap of meat and clung to the tattered remnants of his fur coat, shivering against the cold. Who thought us holy, but perhaps not holy enough not to kill. I bit his head off. It took quite a while. He would not stop talking.

There was the woodsman who thought we ate his chickens. He was stiff, like something out of a fairy tale. He could see us only out of the pages of old ideas. Nothing we could have said would convince him different.

We ate him instead and set his chickens free to show that we could be fair and just. Cooked or uncooked, what's the difference? Do you care?

There was the old biologist in his hovel of a house, eat-

ing stew made of whatever animals he wasn't banding. Setting up his fine-mesh nets full of holes because his brain told him that what the old biologist in his hovel of a house, eating stew made of whatever animals he wasn't banding, did was set up fine-mesh nets full of holes because his brain told him that what the old biologist in his hovel of a house, eating stew made of whatever animals he wasn't banding, set up fine-mesh nets. Full of holes.

We sat down to dinner at the bench, all around him. He had not banded us. He could not eat us. But we had seen the ones he'd crushed underfoot by mistake in his fine-mesh nets. We had seen the ones who when they flew off after banding were too disoriented to evade the predator leaping from above or swooping from below. All the instrumentation of trauma in the old shed. The one that might someday burn down, but that was not our concern.

Our concern was the old biologist, sitting there on the bench eating his weak stew, his tender soup.

"Is it good?" I asked. "Is it fine?"

"It's hearty," he replied, his face a map of his own weakness more than he knew.

In the basement were his attempts at art. Masterpieces some thought, but to us merely the evidence of kidnap victims. Posed normal, noble, not struggled entangled. Not in the shed, splayed out and shoved down. Alien abductions. Blood taken. Probed. Vast and choking light smashed into the huge eyes. Talons held tender yet still held unwilling.

Rates of trauma in re-banded birds. Rates of trauma in old biologists whose research was suspect. Rates of trauma

in drone harassment. Crunch of birds underfoot. But it's a species, not an individual.

The loneliness of the musk ox released back into the herd, forever marked and alone. Taking shelter in the snow, alone. The seal with the glue-affixed beacon on the forehead. Maybe it will come off. Maybe it doesn't matter. Here's a kingfisher. I had to kill it so I could save it. The bighorn sheep that, the last of its herd, looked at the reflection in car metal to know of another of its kind.

"We need data from you," I explained to the old biologist.

He, the object, objected, but we pushed past that point, until the binocular necklace was pressed tight against his throat. We took his blood. We weighed him. We shined bright lights upon his lined face. He didn't understand. How could he? We barely understood ourselves. These rituals, how do they evade scrutiny. How they evade scrutiny. What we tell ourselves is important.

He pissed himself and we took that sample too. Dehydrated, despite the stew. There was too much of the wrong kind of bird in that stew, his nets too poked through with holes, for us to mistake the results of that.

There were monsters in the night. Things that would never be studied. We let the biologist go, out into that darkness, holding his binoculars like a weapon. Swinging them against whatever lay in wait. Watched as he, shrieking, was pulled up into the night, flung and quartered, soon scraps for predators. It wasn't our fault. We needed our data. We had our data. Still, no excuses. We had no control or controls.

"You don't mind if we band you, do you?" I asked. "It's

what we do. We band things. It's nothing personal. It's about the species."

We burned down the nets, burned down the house. Spared the shed. I could not take the echo that I knew was coming to me from somewhere in the future or the past—it wasn't clear.

Our data told us to discontinue that particular experiment, so we did. Instead, we traveled north, our breath fierce in our throats and our eyes encrusted with the white rust of ice.

The furriers who kept our arctic brothers and sisters in tiny pens and then skinned them alive for their fur . . . these furriers we herded off a cliff into an abandoned quarry. A fox can be a sheepdog. A fox can be whatever he wants to be, contrary to legend. Careening crazed around the edges as the furriers pleaded and stumbled even as they ran. Teetered there on the cliff's edge. As long as they could. Toppled and fell in ragged lines of flailing human, falling out of the sky to Earth. The screams ripped from them, battering the rock, reaching not our ears. The last one of them wheeling arms, red-faced, shouting for mercy. If only he had not been clad head to toe in fox, perhaps we could have forgiven a single, a solitary soul. Perhaps, then, seeing the error of his ways, he would have released his prisoners. But we had already done that. And a soul is just a delusion that lives in the body. No delusion survives death. Death is more honest than that.

Broken-limbed at the bottom, split and riven, so the red could leak into the exhausted gravel and turn weeds sodden. Brains dashed out as fast as they'd dashed to the edge. Not

puppets expressed there. No, not puppets. No one could ever use their skins for anything in that condition. But who but a barbarian would wear the skin of his enemy?

I suppose I was, for a time, deranged. The rest are a blur and a burr and a rankle, even now. A tug-tug of direction or misdirection. I cannot rest thinking about them. How the effort was a waste. How not a one could see me. How I could smell and hear them all too clearly. That I knew more about them from their scent than they knew about themselves. That this one was dying of cancer. That that one suffered from a brain tumor. That the rasp of breath wasted on pleading was close to the rasp of death anyway. What did they know about me? Only that I was a demon come to murder them all.

And what was ease but boredom? The tromping clod so quick to track the way they stank like any dead thing as their victims' path took them quick and sure leaping over their bodies into the wilderness beyond. Because our arctic kin distrusted us as much as they distrusted humans; they had seen what we could do.

The way they stank so hard and long it was as if they trailed spirals of fire through the night. The way not one of those liberated would join us, could understand our mission.

A fox is just a prisoner who hasn't escaped yet.

A fox seen in the daytime must have something wrong with it.

A fox is a question that must be answered.

A fox is vermin. Ought to be shot. Quite right. Loose the hounds, my good man. Train them first on the kits, or

the hounds will never learn to kill a full-grown fox. Tally. Tallyho.

A fox is not just a fox is not just a fox.

How tiresome it became, too, for other reasons. Oh, how these dead people who lived in houses on lots where they had cut down most of the trees loved trees. How they loved to be out in the trees. The tales they told about the trees and how they loved them. Perhaps because trees did not resist. Trees fell over of their own accord, sometimes, as if to prove their love of the ax. The chain saw that felled most of them just completed a tree's own inevitable thought.

The proof—that trees never turned chain saws against the ones that wielded them. The chain saws, which were even named, as if they were as alive as a tree, had a personality. Greta. Berta. Charlie. Frank. Sarah. So some we killed with chain saws, to remind them of what it really meant to be a tree. A messy business. Difficult for them and for us.

Absurd of foxes to do all of this. We had no hands. We did not walk upright. We were not made to use human tools. Yet still we did it, and did it well and with vigor.

Do you doubt me? Do you not see the corpses strewn there in my mind's eye? Can you not distinguish truth from fiction? Or were you never taught the difference?

I'm not laughing at you; I'm laughing with you. Except: Foxes don't laugh, they grin. Do you know what a grin from a fox means?

But I was not content to wage such a ragged war upon the enemy. I raised a great liberation army and stood one dusk looking out upon the glittering plain where the humans had camped. They did not know we were their enemy. They had come to that desolate place to battle another army of humans. That was the way of them—to fight each other even as they waged war on us as well. War against us was a casual affair, as quick as thought but without thought.

I stood above that glittering valley, the dusty plain, and watched the legions arrayed there. An army that didn't think of itself as an army. Even as they killed us quick and casual, slow and calculated. Poisoned the darkness with an everlasting and cruel light. They did not smell our blood, heard nothing that we shrieked out or moaned.

We set upon you in the night. And you, bewildered that your quarry should be full of so much rage, as if killing us had been a gift you'd given us. Confused that we fought to the death. That we could overcome the animal instinct to flee, to survive, to subsist.

We stormed the gates. We died in droves. We laid siege. We were destroyed from within and from without. Still, we surged. Still, there were enough of us . . . for a time.

So much I could sense what they could not, even in the middle of battle. The electromagnetic fields were already in my head. The trails left by voles crisscrossed the night

ground, luminous green. I could never be lost, held tight that way by the world. There was no darkness for me, no light.

Yet still I lost, because I was being human.

Killing is easy. I think that's why people do it so much.

But soon I realized the error. I was just doing what had been done to me and mine. Revenge was not sweet. Revenge deformed. I saw my mistake and I atoned because I had been bad, revolutionary turned terrorist. Soon I was on the march with my army again—this time rebuilding what we had destroyed, helping humans repair their cities, restore their lights, their shops, their vehicles. And they were thankful. They thanked us as they always had, for we had misunderstood, thought that they did not love us. But of course they loved us, because they said they did.

No, that's not it. That's not what happened. Who could in their hearts forgive mass murderers? It's that it still wasn't *enough*. There were too many of you and too few of us. I could kill you from sunrise to sunset and it would never be enough.

Still, I tried. I attended social events. I observed and thought about what I saw. At a masquerade, a cocktail party. On another Earth, where still you humans congregated at public institutions and people's houses to drink and talk because there were institutions because there still were houses. If I could kill humans, I could disguise myself as one to mingle. Mingling was a big thing for humans. To show off houses. To show off wealth. Like marking things was for us.

This house had a slow death of useless objects on its walls. This house stank of toxic house cleaners and the food stank of pesticides and the people stank of pesticides, too, but didn't know it. I didn't have to kill any of them; most were dying of cancer, slowly, and didn't know it. Most had bellies full of plastic. The plastic would grow and grow in their bellies until, years from now, as they mingled, as they drank expensive wine, their bellies would burst and out would come all the plastic, dribbling onto the floor. Pressing cool and bloody against some synthetic floor. Plastic in love with synthetic. Pressing there cool and bloody. Finally home.

Businessmen mingled at this party. They mingled with artists who made them amazing sculptures of abstract animals and cute animals. The owner of the house loved the ironic taxidermy of roadkill. "If it's roadkill, it's pure. I just make them beautiful again." The taxidermist was there.

I wondered if I ran over the taxidermist and preserved her in resin if she would feel beautiful. If she would feel pure. Exploded first into a jagged eruption and pulling apart of flesh and tissue and bone and sinew. Left with a hole where the chest had been. A face half sawed off. Or perhaps a broken back, still alive and gasping, but crushed to asphalt in the middle, hoping now for another car to finish the carnage.

But, to mingle. I must mingle. I must hover and flit and pirouette and make my excuses to the next conversation and engage in small talk.

"What about the weather?" But you could not talk about the weather on this Earth. The weather had turned bad. The weather was a traitor.

“What about sports?” But you could not talk about sports because the weather had “fucked up” the sports.

What could we talk about? I complimented the owners on their house. My voice had a rasp to it, then. I wasn’t yet comfortable talking human. My voice had a rasp, and I gazed upon the bison head on the wall and my voice became raspier still. I gazed upon the mossy rock imported from another country, the water feature in the house, and wanted only to return to all fours and to drink from the pond. To gaze at my reflection and remember who I was, not what I had become.

“Did you find that here or did you have to go online?”

“That tablecloth created by forced labor looks amazing on that table manufactured with formaldehyde in a sweatshop.”

“Do you have the new phone yet that someone made continents away because they were forced to and then someone else starved to death because when they mined the components they destroyed all the crop lands and the forest?”

It was bracing to hear such honest talk, even if only in my head.

“And what do you do?” Directed at me.

The rasp: “I’m in private equality.”

“Equity?”

“Equality.”

“Wolves all in equity.”

“Some of them are foxes,” I said.

Then I revealed myself and my emissaries came smashing through the special nonreflective glass that had stopped

birds from flying into it even as the owners' vehicles and leaf blowers and pesticides had poisoned all the birds into extinction.

There is a question I should ask, but I feel you've forgotten the answer. I feel there's no point in asking now.

What do you run in? Do you run in? Do you ever run in circles chasing your own tail? Is your tail ever on fire yet you chase it still? Circles. Reentry. Burning up like a space capsule. Fever run hot. Why lunge for a jugular when you could rip out tendons, watch the timber fall, and then, at your leisure, circle back in the dark.

Sometimes it wasn't about the hunt or the kill. Sometimes it was about meting out in equal measure a never-ending bile. A never-endingness. A never-ending moment of never having rest. Let them never rest as they have not allowed us to rest, to just be. May they always be on the run, looking over their shoulder, that we may have peace.

It wasn't a cabin. It was a burrow. We knew they'd come for us. But we could see what they couldn't. We knew, and by the time they arrived, we weren't there. Or we were underfoot, underneath—under the pine needles, the bramble, the dirt, even the limestone. We could hear them above, clumsy, loud. But we had dissipated. We had dissolved like rainwater into the substrate.

To hide, I came back to my own. Through all the hidden doorways. I spread myself thin to do so. I made many

versions of myself. We multiplied through the burrows. We came out the other end . . . different. In different places.

I watched—

I watched *a* Grayson on *an* empty moon base. Frozen there. Unable to decide. For that Grayson, I became the noise around the corner that made her blanch, made her decision for her. In another it was the hatching sound of a thousand Company invertebrates, which had swept the base clean. Maybe in a third, Grayson left for simple loneliness and the Company never reached that moon.

I watched—

I watched—

I came back to my own. I bled through mud. I fell in sand and dirt. I ate lichen off old stone and dead tree trunk. I snapped up mice again. Rolled in yellow grass and offal. Still they did not know me as kin. I smelled wretched, like you, not like fox. I could not shed it. I was an alien, come down from the stars to them. I wished it wasn't so. I wished I could run with them. Remember nothing. Be erased under the moon. Disappear into Nocturnalia.

But still I came back to them. I came back to their minds through their scent. They sniffed me and danced around me and I was still not like me. Not like them.

Yet they stayed and followed me.

You say why save an empty Earth? I can smell it on you, hear it in your voice. The way you can't remember because how could you live. But it's only empty to your eyes. It's only empty because you helped make it so, and thought nothing of it.

There is no end to us. Only to you. You'll never under-

stand that. You'll never understand that without us, you don't exist. You wink out of existence. You become something else. Forever. And when I'm gone, what will remain? Everything.

Everything will remain.

iii.

to the children i loved

We lived in joy, the joy of living without interference, without persecution, without unnatural threat. The joy of running. The joy of digging. The joy of hunting earthworms through the dirt. The joy of the wind against fur. The joy of muddy paws. The joy of sleeping next to mate and kits. The joy of climbing trees. The joy of swimming in streams. The joy of mating and raising children. The joy of digging burrows. The joy of playing in meadows. The joy of snapping at fireflies at dusk. The joy of napping on smooth stones, on moss, on beds of ferns. The joy of the warmth on fur. We lived in joy, the joy of living without interference, without persecution, without unnatural threat.

The joy of running. The joy of digging. The joy of hunting earthworms through the dirt. The joy of the wind against fur. The joy of muddy paws. The joy of sleeping next to mate and kits. The joy of climbing trees. The joy of swimming in streams. The joy of mating and raising children. The joy of digging burrows. The joy of playing in meadows. The joy of snapping at fireflies at dusk. The joy of napping on smooth stones, on moss, on beds of ferns. The joy of the warmth on fur. We lived in joy, the joy of living without interference, without persecution, without unnatural threat. The joy of running. The joy of digging. The joy of hunting earthworms through the dirt. The joy of the wind against fur. The joy of muddy paws. The joy of sleeping next to mate and kits. The joy of climbing trees. The joy of swimming in streams. The joy of mating and raising children. The joy of digging burrows. The joy of playing in meadows. The joy of snapping at fireflies at dusk. The joy of napping on smooth stones, on moss, on beds of ferns. The joy of the warmth on fur. We lived in joy, the joy of living without interference, without persecution, without unnatural threat. The joy of running. The joy of digging. The joy of hunting earthworms through the dirt. The joy of the wind against fur. The joy of muddy paws. The joy of sleeping next to mate and kits. The joy of climbing trees. The joy of swimming in streams. The joy of mating and raising children. The joy of digging burrows. The joy of playing in meadows. The joy of snapping at fireflies at dusk. The joy of napping on smooth stones, on moss, on beds of ferns. The joy of the warmth on fur. We lived in joy, the joy of living without interference, without persecution, without unnatural threat.

The joy of running. The joy of digging. The joy of hunting earthworms through the dirt. The joy of the wind against fur. The joy of muddy paws. The joy of sleeping next to mate and kits. The joy of climbing trees. The joy of swimming in streams. The joy of mating and raising children. The joy of digging burrows. The joy of playing in meadows. The joy of snapping at fireflies at dusk. The joy of napping on smooth stones, on moss, on beds of ferns. The joy of the warmth on fur. We lived in joy, the joy of living without interference, without persecution, without unnatural threat. The joy of running. The joy of digging. The joy of hunting earthworms through the dirt. The joy of the wind against fur. The joy of muddy paws. The joy of sleeping next to mate and kits. The joy of climbing trees. The joy of swimming in streams. The joy of mating and raising children. The joy of digging burrows. The joy of playing in meadows. The joy of snapping at fireflies at dusk. The joy of napping on smooth stones, on moss, on beds of ferns. The joy of the warmth on fur. We lived in joy, the joy of living without interference, without persecution, without unnatural threat. The joy of running. The joy of digging. The joy of hunting earthworms through the dirt. The joy of the wind against fur. The joy of muddy paws. The joy of sleeping next to mate and kits. The joy of climbing trees. The joy of swimming in streams. The joy of mating and raising children. The joy of digging burrows. The joy of playing in meadows. The joy of snapping at fireflies at dusk. The joy of napping on smooth stones, on moss, on beds of ferns. The joy of the warmth on fur. We lived in joy, the joy of living without interference, without persecution, without unnatural threat.

The joy of running. The joy of digging. The joy of hunting earthworms through the dirt. The joy of the wind against fur. The joy of muddy paws. The joy of sleeping next to mate and kits. The joy of climbing trees. The joy of swimming in streams. The joy of mating and raising children. The joy of digging burrows. The joy of playing in meadows. The joy of snapping at fireflies at dusk. The joy of napping on smooth stones, on moss, on beds of ferns. The joy of the warmth on fur. We lived in joy, the joy of living without interference, without persecution, without unnatural threat. The joy of running. The joy of digging. The joy of hunting earthworms through the dirt. The joy of the wind against fur. The joy of muddy paws. The joy of sleeping next to mate and kits. The joy of climbing trees. The joy of swimming in streams. The joy of mating and raising children. The joy of digging burrows. The joy of playing in meadows. The joy of snapping at fireflies at dusk. The joy of napping on smooth stones, on moss, on beds of ferns. The joy of the warmth on fur. We lived in joy, the joy of living without interference, without persecution, without unnatural threat. (While we felt it in the soil and danced on dead leaves and rutted and drank at the stream that ran behind the row of apartments and watched the sun, that radiant star, and kept the island in our hearts.) The joy of running. The joy of digging. The joy of hunting earthworms through the dirt. The joy of the wind against fur. The joy of muddy paws. The joy of sleeping next to mate and kits. The joy of climbing trees. The joy of swimming in streams. The joy of mating and raising children. The joy of digging burrows. (Knew that we would return there, if we lived that long.) The joy of playing

in meadows. The joy of snapping at fireflies at dusk. The joy of napping on smooth stones, on moss, on beds of ferns. The joy of the warmth on fur. We lived in joy, the joy of living without interference, without persecution, without unnatural threat. (If we could just outlast, outcast.) The joy of running. The joy of digging. The joy of hunting earthworms through the dirt. The joy of the wind against fur. The joy of muddy paws. The joy of sleeping next to mate and kits. The joy of climbing trees. The joy of swimming in streams. The joy of mating and raising children. The joy of digging burrows. The joy of playing in meadows. The joy of snapping at fireflies at dusk. The joy of napping on smooth stones, on moss, on beds of ferns. The joy of the warmth on fur. We lived in joy, the joy of living without interference, without persecution, without unnatural threat. The joy of running. The joy of digging. The joy of hunting earthworms through the dirt. The joy of the wind against fur. The joy of muddy paws. The joy of sleeping next to mate and kits. The joy of climbing trees. The joy of swimming in streams. The joy of mating and raising children. The joy of digging burrows. The joy of playing in meadows. The joy of snapping at fireflies at dusk. The joy of napping on smooth stones, on moss, on beds of ferns. The joy of the warmth on fur. We lived in joy, the joy of living without interference, without persecution, without unnatural threat. The joy of running. The joy of digging. The joy of hunting earthworms through the dirt. The joy of the wind against fur. The joy of muddy paws. The joy of sleeping next to mate and kits. The joy of climbing trees. The joy of swimming in streams. The joy of mating and raising children. The joy of

digging burrows. The joy of playing in meadows. The joy of snapping at fireflies at dusk. The joy of napping on smooth stones, on moss, on beds of ferns. The joy of the warmth on fur. We lived in joy, the joy of living without interference, without persecution, without unnatural threat. The joy of running. The joy of digging. The joy of hunting earthworms through the dirt. The joy of the wind against fur. The joy of muddy paws. The joy of sleeping next to mate and kits. The joy of climbing trees. The joy of swimming in streams. The joy of mating and raising children. The joy of digging burrows. The joy of playing in meadows. The joy of snapping at fireflies at dusk. The joy of napping on smooth stones, on moss, on beds of ferns. The joy of the warmth on fur. We lived in joy, the joy of living without interference, without persecution, without unnatural threat. The joy of running. The joy of digging. The joy of hunting earthworms through the dirt. The joy of the wind against fur. The joy of muddy paws. The joy of sleeping next to mate and kits. The joy of climbing trees. The joy of swimming in streams. The joy of mating and raising children. The joy of digging burrows. The joy of playing in meadows. The joy of snapping at fireflies at dusk. The joy of napping on smooth stones, on moss, on beds of ferns. The joy of the warmth on fur. (Did I see you through the bramble? Once or twice. Did I sneak up to the edge of the forest to surveil the factory?) We lived in joy, the joy of living without interference, without persecution, without unnatural threat. The joy of running. The joy of digging. The joy of hunting earthworms through the dirt. The joy of the wind against fur. The joy of muddy paws.

The joy of sleeping next to mate and kits. The joy of climbing trees. The joy of swimming in streams. The joy of mating and raising children. The joy of digging burrows. The joy of playing in meadows. The joy of snapping at fireflies at dusk. The joy of napping on smooth stones, on moss, on beds of ferns. The joy of the warmth on fur. We lived in joy, the joy of living without interference, without persecution, without unnatural threat. The joy of running. The joy of digging. The joy of hunting earthworms through the dirt. The joy of the wind against fur. The joy of muddy paws. The joy of sleeping next to mate and kits. The joy of climbing trees. The joy of swimming in streams. The joy of mating and raising children. The joy of digging burrows. The joy of playing in meadows. The joy of snapping at fireflies at dusk. The joy of napping on smooth stones, on moss, on beds of ferns. The joy of the warmth on fur. (Did I watch the dark bird at its work but do nothing? And was I a ghost? Was I so far away I could do nothing anyway? For what was to be done? Nothing.) We lived in joy, the joy of living without interference, without persecution, without unnatural threat. The joy of running. The joy of digging. The joy of hunting earthworms through the dirt. The joy of the wind against fur. The joy of muddy paws. The joy of sleeping next to mate and kits. The joy of climbing trees. The joy of swimming in streams. The joy of mating and raising children. The joy of digging burrows. The joy of playing in meadows. The joy of snapping at fireflies at dusk. The joy of napping on smooth stones, on moss, on beds of ferns. The joy of the warmth on fur.

But, in the end, joy cannot fend off evil.
Joy can only remind you why you fight.

It was not always you, here, in this room, with me half dead hanging from the wall. Once, it was them, and far away. The ones who took me. Where did they take me from? The usual places. The ones you don't understand because you don't really see them. You live there, but you could live anywhere.

My life wasn't much. Before. Not to you. To you it would be strange and over-silent and made of blank spaces and space too long. The wrong gait and the wrong gate. A fence where I see none. Or none not defeated by a leap.

I was the tree fox, the water fox, never meant for the desert. When happiest I lived on an island within swimming distance of the mainland. A copse. A sullen stream, weary of summer people tossing garbage in it. A stream clogged with rocks, the kind where you pry up the moss and find delicious crayfish. I liked to jump onto a river rock. Sit there

as the sun washed through the trees and through the water. The sudden regard of it. How it spread out to cover us and I could sense the growth and decay of all around me.

The sun was a star. I knew that, even then. I knew we live on a planet. I can sense magnetic fields. I can feel the weight of the Earth turning. I can listen to the networks between trees and view their own map of constellations. So I knew better than you. Better than books.

I had a mate and we had children and we raised them well and then they left to strike out on their own and would raise more. We would live in caves and dens and abandoned buildings overgrown with vines. Always near a river. Always near the basking stones.

There was no moment like any other moment and yet each moment was the same.

We slept in trees, on branches thick with moss and ferns. That was our bed. We would sleep in the heat, and rise to play and sit in the sun and hunt rabbits and mice. We would explore the heart of abandoned towns fallen again to weeds and bramble. We would paw past the ashes of cold campgrounds. We were bold and loud often and did not care, especially at night.

The thing we didn't know, child. But felt. The reason we began to look forward to a time we could be truly careless: It was the end, not the middle, the end not the beginning. The time of your kind was ending. We knew it in the busy places that became still, watchful. We knew it in how fewer lights shone at night and how more shadows we sniffed were stray dogs. (Oh, stray dogs were a bumbling marvel, even the best and keenest of them! For we had changed.)

Still, you took things from us. Even then. Became more ferocious as you disappeared, as if you knew it in your hearts.

You burnt part of the forest on the island. We moved to the mainland. We lived in gardens. You cut down the verge. We lived in the shadow of lawns. You filled in the lawns with gravel. We lived on rooftops. You could not take sky; we kept that for ourselves and the tunnels below, too. So that humans were garlanded by us and yet never saw us.

But we saw you.

Maybe, once, from afar, once there was a bridge and a poisoned river. Maybe once in our travels we passed by that which once had been beset by fire. Maybe we knew. Maybe I knew what it might come to mean.

We became careless and yet were not killed. By snare. By bullet. By poison. Because there had been a person always to kill us. Now the people truly became a murmur across the land. A puzzled, bewildered muttering.

I was wary-wise and soft-new, naïve back then. I would have growled and yipped at you, or you would have known nothing of me, even if I stood close, in the shadows, and I would have been better for it. Perhaps.

Then one day I was taken and I became the blue fox.

There was an insect up above. A drone that hovered, made of flesh and metal. I remember I stood on my hind legs to see it better. How it shone in the sun!

The men came much later. A shadow. A metallic smell

appearing as if magician-summoned. A sound from an old abandoned building that had always been safe before. The pale men that always come before the end, that signal the invasion. And the locals they enlisted. The banal drawling drowning speech of men who don't care about what they're doing. Until forced to. Who all unawares destroy their own warrens, who poison their own food, convinced of righteousness.

I should have been wary. There is nothing you cannot hear if the world is quiet enough. And if the world will not be silent, you will have to make yourself silent. So silent. That all the sound everywhere means nothing. But still I did not hear, not on that day. Fell into the trap. Fell into the floor in the bottom of the world, tumbling into the dark, out on the other side in someone else's warren.

There came the piercing thread of agony in the shoulder. There came the dizziness, the stagger, the fall into leaves and moss, amid the snails and earthworms. Down close where the earth smells like heaven.

My mate watched from the bushes. She knew she couldn't save me, and I didn't want her to try. Still I saw her. As I faded. As I faded into becoming something else, not new or old. As they took me away. Still looking into her eyes.

The sentimental tale. The tale you always need to care. Which shows you don't care. Why we don't care if you care.

Once, I went to the farthest extreme, to the very edge of the realities, pushed up against the impossible. I was sick with my power, besotted with it. I thought no place had a fence I could not dig under or jump over. Or that no place defended by a fence might be dangerous. My mind was a feral place and strange creatures darted through it in the night. And I welcomed them.

Beyond where the Company had ever wanted me to go. More than they had wanted me to see. Perhaps it was the past, not the future. Perhaps all the answers lay in the past, or maybe time did not move as we thought it did. That our movement was a kind of reality or world all by itself. Ever the numbers that bound it and made it so: the three, the countdown from ten, the seven, with their dozens of fragments.

Limitless, I came to a world where the moon lay so huge and ivory and cratered that it blotted out the sun above a mirror-twin to Earth. Except, there in that strange land everything was alive and nothing was dead, even the dead, and I could find no familiar scent to guide me through. Where the rocks spoke to me and so did the water and so did the sand and so did the plants.

There, ultimately, I found my purpose. There, I was transformed once more and truly became the blue fox. Out where all the smells run together and you cannot trust your senses.

What lived there had lost its name long ago. What lived there changed shape and form and spoke in different voices. Had been created as one thing, brought up as another. What lived there was serious and playful and lonely but not

alone. It had known me before. It knew me now, read my mind, my intent, encouraged it.

"It will take time. You will not survive to see the end of it. And one day, Time will bring you back here, in some form. To this place."

"How do you know this?"

But there was just laughter in reply.

In the end, if you change the enemy enough, if you wear them down, perhaps losing is good enough.

This much I know, among all the other things I know.

Once upon a time, I spoke to three dead astronauts. Past, present, future? All so proud, so determined. All so doomed. They told me their plans. They were so pure. They did not ask me about my past, where I had come from. Not in the right way. They did not imagine I might be similar to them. But I was the one sent where no one else wanted to go. I understood them better than they knew.

I could talk like Grayson now. Or Chen. Or maybe even Moss. I could claim to conjure with leviathans or through great bears and salamanders. I could bark at you. I could be silent and hurt you in the dark by smell alone. By the sounds you careless left behind you.

Perhaps you were right to pin me alive to this wall as trophy and warning both. Even if the magician who did it is just the dying fall, a living ruin. I escaped. But, of course,

a human found me eventually. Some human. Didn't care what I was up to. Didn't remember what I'd done. Cut off my head. Stuck me up on this observatory wall. Could have been any human.

I couldn't protect my children. Couldn't protect my mate. She couldn't protect me. History didn't allow for that. History had other plans. Don't know if the need is part of me or part of them. The pool of water. The stream. The salamanders there. There tasty earthworms. The burrow. All of us together, in the burrow.

They have been dead three hundred years now.

I should be dead with them. A fox lives four years.

I must not be a fox anymore.

They killed me. They brought me back.

One time I escaped. But it was too late.

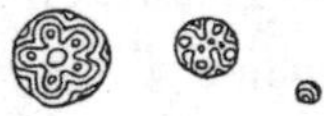

The ghosts come out at night, child. Except here they are not really ghosts but the eyes of this place. In the silent hall, under the broken dome, when all of you lie asleep, fallen where you will in your fatigue, waiting to be resurrected in the morning. Then the ghost images. In a spectrum of light you cannot see. The history of this place, recollected: Held by some for a time. Driven out. Another group replacing them. Such repetition for so long, the only difference in the details of the conquest, the defeat.

But all along at dusk, in the shadows, my kind slinking through. My kind emerging from the tunnels below. The

ones you never saw, making our own history, creating our own lives. Unrecorded.

And me, nailed to the wall, neither alive nor quite yet dead. I look down Charlie X as the ghosts move through him, look down upon the human shadows as the past becomes brazen in that space. Violence here happened so long ago, the motion of the past come to life like some long dance no one realized they were part of. I wonder if killing you would have been better than slinking nocturnal, but, then, you killed yourselves anyway. We just needed to survive long enough, sacrifice more. Charlie X was never pragmatic like a fox, never aware like a fox.

Sometimes this resurrection is peaceful in its way, because the violence in it happened so long ago. I feel this way when the need to rest comes over me. The motion of all the past come to life is like some long dance the dancers don't realize is in motion. Even the killing. Even the strife. So silent in this place. So still. In the end.

The irony that I am changed enough, child. Changed that much. That I must tell this to you. Must snare your mind in it, in the hope that, someday, you'll see a fox or a track and you'll write it all down. You'll pass it down somehow. That somehow it will matter.

But that will never happen. I won't have to rely on that. You'll grow old or you won't. But one day or night, you'll lay your head down to sleep and you won't wake up and in time, through worm and fly, through scavenger and rot . . . your skull will be laid bare, and there, on the bone, they'll find my story, not yours.

This story. From the beginning.

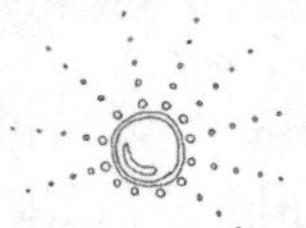

A blinding blue star over the desert, shining down on all. Shining down for just a moment. Shining down eternal.

Now I see it all as I recede and become nothing but a pelt nailed to a wall. Now I see. I see, from so long ago, my mate, my children. I see them playful along the river's edge. Watching them from a cool, flat stone. The play of water against rock. The dappled tree-tumbled sunlight of centuries ago. Worlds ago.

Feel the edges of the rough-cool burrow. Where I'll dig deep and go to ground. Rest in the cool earth, in the comfortable dark. A fox knows how to hide. A fox, through the generations, knows how to wait.

And one day, finally, I will be free.

10. THE DEAD ASTRONAUT

v.7.0

The compass that does not know its name. The map that does not know its borders. The journey in search of a destination.

The dead astronaut at the coast. Her legs are weary and her feet sore. She can see out of only one eye. The other sees things that aren't there. She has pain in her shoulder and a constant ache in her knees.

It has taken years, not months. She has been waylaid by enemies she could not have known. From the sky, from beneath the earth. Thrown off course, although she has defeated everyone: killed or run or hid. Driven her blade deep or cowered in shadows as a great bulk prowled past. Her gun long since useless, discarded, a shadow on the sands behind her.

The ocean breeze broken by the sandy ridge ahead,

rippling so gentle against her face it feels like a kindness offered up as cruelty. The sharp, sudden brine of it, which makes her want to salivate, though her mouth is desolate.

She is hollow, hollowed out, black skin tinged gray with ash, gray stubble of hair blackened by smoke. Her throat so dry, hands cracked and calloused. So close now that she weeps without tears from the relief of it. To come to an end. Some sort of ending. Her body trembles with emotion she can no longer identify.

The woman who trudges up the ridge, the dune, has been reduced and sharpened by lack. Of water of food of companionship. Reduced to talking to the dark birdlike drones that circle high above but hasten down to rule her out as threat. Sharpened by the collapse that makes the landscape a reflection of how she feels on the inside.

Sanded down to only what is required to move one foot and then the next ahead, toward the coast. Need narrowed to a point and *want* exiled to another country.

Only now did she know who she was.

Would her voice work? It would crackle, would seem like it issued forth from a mouth full of rust.

The limitless, searing blue blinds her for a moment.

At the top of the dune, the dead astronaut trembles, stands tender and useless. Her rags are loose, torn and tearing and flapping in the wind. Teeters, wants to fall. Doesn't.

Before her lies a thin strip of remembered beach, gold flecked with black, then a calm bay of still water, dark blue, strewn with kelp beds and deep rock pools.

Presented ethereal. Presented as naïve, with green eyes that blazed. Before that gaze the horizon is limitless again.

Yet: There is no sign of ruins. There is not, on this coast, the half-fallen arch of a marine park. No landmark she can recall.

Hesitation. Lingering regard on what is still distant through a preamble of sand and stickery plants.

Is that movement down on the rocks? She cannot spare the attention yet. She cannot afford the answer. Instead, she focuses on putting one foot after the other down the dune, bent at the knees.

One foot and then the next. Looking down at her ragged torn shoes held together with bloody bandages she took off a dead man.

Then she is on the beach, the rough gravel feel of this sand, so different from the smooth heat of the desert.

Now the dead astronaut must look up from her feet. Now she must face what isn't there. What is there.

The tremor inside isn't perceptible on the dead astronaut's face. But it is seismic, and she is quivering in a way that she's afraid she can't stop.

A figure out in the tidal pools, faced away from her. Bending over in observation of something in those depths. The sun hides the figure, gives sanctuary against the dead astronaut's parched gaze. She shields her eyes with a shaking hand. She still cannot tell.

It might be no one. No one she knew. It might not matter. Some trick, some final joke the blue fox was playing on her, all these years later. Something the fox wanted her to see through negation, through want, still wandering in the fox's mind.

Would there be recognition or the awful blankness of

deep space reflected back? Never left the moon base. Never took the chance to plunge back down to Earth, to seek out a happiness she never imagined would be open to her.

A trick of the light, and after she would wander down the coast, lost. She would wander until she fell and never rise again.

It takes her final courage to continue. To walk to the edge of the rocks, the figure still unaware. The dead astronaut staring at her reflection in the tidal pools, as if it might hurt to stare direct.

All the beautiful things in those tidal pools. That the Company might never know. Never touch. Not to infiltrate, the dead astronaut can tell. But to build something new, something that might last. How they would remain in the sea. How they might flourish, might multiply. But: How strange and delicate and wise. A loving God nurturing them. A God who would know enough to disappear in time.

The figure straightens up, stiffens, must know someone watches. The figure is wrapped in robes, the hair short, not like the dead astronaut remembered. The figure turns, and even then the sun occludes the features.

The dead astronaut is something inanimate, no better than the piles of driftwood, except they have come to rest. But she will not look away.

The figure approaches, comes out of the sun into a different light.

Can it be true?

She doubts, she doubts so much because if it is not, then what was it for? Any of it? Suffers from how much she has forgotten of her love that she should doubt.

"Do you know me?" she says to the woman who stands before her. She doesn't even know if she's said words. She is trembling at the brightness of everything around her, how it infiltrates and sees through her. How it knows her as nothing has known her for years.

"Moss?"

There is something unfamiliar in the face that makes the dead astronaut ask. A focus or intent that did not live in memory.

"My name is Sarah," the woman says. "Not Moss."

The dead astronaut's face must betray her.

"Sarah." This time firmer. The blaze of those green eyes, the certainty that lives there.

Awful. A void. An abyss. Stumbling, falling, hands cut open on the edge of coral and of rock. But welcoming the pain, the sight of blood, the cool, cold mouths of water.

Then the woman is beside her, holding her up, the touch more familiar than the voice.

"I'm sorry. I'm sorry. I must look . . . I didn't mean to . . ." Babbling, gone. So far gone. Yet also, beneath it, the relief of simple human contact.

"How far have you traveled? To be in such a state?"

The dead astronaut lets out a sharp, thready laugh. "Not far. Not far."

"And your friend, Moss . . . she lived here?"

"Once upon a time. Somewhen."

“She meant a lot to you.” It isn’t a question.

The dead astronaut nods. She cannot see inside Sarah’s head. It’s a strange feeling, a numbness but also a relief.

“And I look like her?” Sarah’s voice puzzled, like she’s working on a riddle.

“You do.”

A hesitation, Sarah weighing some risk.

Then she embraces the dead astronaut, soft but tight. Doesn’t have to, the dead astronaut knows that. Knows all of that. Resists, tries to pull away, then relaxes, clings. No strength left for being strong.

“Let me get you something to eat. And water,” Sarah says. “Stay here. I’ll be back.”

Disengages, and the dead astronaut tries not to hang on, to retain some sense of self. Not to cling to each footfall leading away from there. Must trust.

Waits there as the water teases and gasps through the rocks. As some lonely bird drifts off the coast, joined by a second. As the wind against her face intensifies.

Oh, my love, what will I do without you?

Everything and nothing.

Yet there is still so much of Moss here, in the tidal pools, so much of Moss in Sarah. All the strange life there. The ache of that, and yet, pushing it away, the thought that perhaps if put out of sight, out of mind, some new thing might grow.

Somewhere there might be a Grayson who perished in the desert, without hope. Somewhere there might be a Grayson who never found even a Sarah. Somewhere there might be a Grayson who suffered less, who held on to more.

But she was the dead astronaut and she lay merciful somewhere between those points on the compass and always would.

Grayson come to rest, unable to move after so long in motion. Shuddering with the aftershock of Sarah's embrace. Which, even unawares, could convey so much and withhold nothing. The joy of life. The joy of living without interference. Without persecution. Without unnatural threat. Without. If she was allowed to think of joy.

History would go on without her, the Company and the foxes, and all the rest. And yet on it went. Their quest, in some form. Even without them. The future would still be the future, in some form. Until the dead astronaut grew old. Or until the end of the world. Whichever came first.

Grayson lay back against the wet sand, staring up at the cloudless sky. There, by the edge of the sea.

Chen stood in the surf, looking out at the waves. She could see him with her bad eye. Had always been able to see him. Her hand in her pocket, wrapped around the scrap of paper Chen had left behind. Should she give it back to him? Should she read it? Or just hold it, tight, in her grip? The words long since faded into nothing. The compacted feel of the paper. The dry rough feel across thousands and thousands of miles.

We will always be there. Even before we know you.

Even after we've known you. Even then.

And, finally, she was free.

0. A SCRAP OF PAPER FOUND IN CHEN'S SUIT v.0

came unto the city
under an evil star

they needed no fire
for the fire burned
within all of them
for you cannot give us
what we already have

the first glimpse
was always the most fatal
no one should feel responsible
for the whole world

by these signs
they knew they were home

the way his face yet reflected
nothing of terrible experience
like two trying
to become one

a shadow
of a vastness
such savage mockery
of the sea

to take the measure of its creator
who no longer remembered the creation

disposable and finite
and vulnerable
to be both receiver
and received

the sickness found
in the midst of beauty
for the price paid for the wonders
within was too high

the coded sky and the scaffolding
the burning speed and the stillness

neither the same again
neither could ever be the same
again

when i am weak
then i am strong
reentry like death
found in flame

beneath the stars
beneath the planets

alone
not alone
never alone

this failure
no failure
for love